FIGHTING WORDS

"Get out of here!" Harper snapped harshly. "Don't come around here again, aimin' to make trouble. That's all you came for, and you know it! You've been looking for an excuse to start something so you could get us out of here, take our homes away from us. Now turn your horses and get out!"

"This is a bad mistake, Harper," Rock said evenly. "I'm speaking of it before all these people." He nodded at the group in front of the house. "Bishop was inclined to let 'em stay, despite the fact that he was afraid they'd bring more after them. He listened to me and didn't run you off. Now you're asking for it."

"He listened to *you!*" Harper's voice was alive with contempt. "You? A trail runner?"

Red looked quickly at Rock and started to speak. Bannon silenced him with a gesture.

"We'll ride, Harper, but we want the man…or men…who killed Wes. And we want him delivered to us by sundown tomorrow. If not, we'll come and get him."

Turning abruptly, they started away. Wheeling, Zapata grabbed a shotgun from one of the teamsters. "I'll fix him, the bluffer!"

Other *Leisure* books by Louis L'Amour:

A MAN CALLED TRENT
THE SIXTH SHOTGUN
THE GOLDEN WEST (Anthology)
THE UNTAMED WEST (Anthology)

LOUIS L'AMOUR

SHOWDOWN TRAIL

LEISURE BOOKS

NEW YORK CITY

A LEISURE BOOK®

March 2007

Published by special arrangement with Golden West Literary Agency.

Dorchester Publishing Co., Inc.
200 Madison Avenue
New York, NY 10016

ISBN 0-8439-5786-7

Printed in the United States of America.

SHOWDOWN TRAIL

TABLE OF CONTENTS

EDITOR'S NOTE

Very early in his career as a pulp writer, in the period just prior to the outbreak of the Second World War, Louis L'Amour created a series character named Pongo Jim Mayo, the master of a tramp steamer in Far Eastern waters, in L'Amour's words "an Irish-American who had served his first five years at sea sailing out of Liverpool and along the west coast of Africa's Pongo River, where he picked up his nickname. He's a character I created from having gotten to know men just like him while I was a seaman in my yondering days." After the war, when L'Amour began to specialize in Western fiction, he wrote most frequently under the pseudonym Jim Mayo, taking it from this early fictional character. "The Trail to Peach Meadow Cañon" by Jim Mayo appeared in *Giant Western* (10/49). It was subsequently reprinted under this same title and byline in *Triple Western* (Fall, '56). The text was expanded and substantially changed when it subsequently was published as an original paperback titled *Son of a Wanted Man* in 1984.

"Showdown Trail" by Jim Mayo first appeared in *Giant Western* (Winter, '48). L'Amour subsequently reworked and expanded this story into *The Tall Stranger*, published as an original paperback in 1957. The expanded story was filmed as *The Tall Stranger* (Allied Artists, 1957) directed by Thomas Carr and starring Joel McCrea and Virginia Mayo.

There is a special magic in these original short novels as they first appeared in their magazine versions, and the texts of both have been scrupulously restored. It has been a pleasure for me to have gathered these fine Western stories together for the first time in book form.

The Trail to Peach Meadow Cañon

Chapter One

Winter snows were melting in the forests of the Kaibab, and the red-and-orange hue of the 1,000-foot Vermilion Cliffs was streaked with the dampness of melting frost. Deer were feeding in the forest glades among the stands of ponderosa and fir, and the trout were leaping in the streams. Where sunlight trailed through the webbed overhang of the leaves, the water danced and sparkled.

Five deer were feeding on the grass along a mountain stream back of Finger Butte, their coats mottled by the light and shadow of the sun shining through the trees. A vague something moved in the woods behind them, and the five-pronged buck lifted his regal head and stared curiously about. He turned his nose into the wind, reading it cautiously. But his trust was betrayal, for the movement was downwind of him.

The movement came again, and a young man stepped from concealment behind a huge fir not twenty feet from the nearest deer. He was straight and tall in gray, fringed buckskins, and he wore no hat. His hair was thick, black, and wavy, growing fully over the temples, and his face was lean and brown. Smiling, he walked toward the deer with quick, lithe strides, and had taken three full steps before some tiny sound betrayed him.

The buck's head came up and swung around, and then with a startled snort it sprang away, the others following.

Mike Bastian stood grinning, his hands on his hips.

"Well, what do you think now, Roundy?" he called. "Could your Apache beat that? I could have touched him if I had jumped after him!"

Rance Roundy came out of the trees—a lean, wiry old man with a gray mustache and blue eyes that were still bright with an alert awareness.

"No, I'll be darned if any Apache ever lived as could beat that!" he chortled. "Not a mite of it! An' I never seen the day I could beat it, either. You're a caution, Mike, you sure are. I'm glad you're not sneakin' up after my hair!" He drew his pipe from his pocket and started stoking it with tobacco. "We're goin' back to Toadstool Cañon, Mike. Your dad sent for us."

Bastian looked up quickly. "Is there trouble, is that it?"

"No, only he wants to talk with you. Maybe"—Roundy was cautious—"he figures it's time you went out on a job. On one of those rides."

"I think that's it." Mike nodded. "He said in the spring, and it's about time for the first ride. I wonder where they'll go this time."

"No tellin'. The deal will be well planned, though. That dad of yours would have made a fine general, Mike. He's got the head for it, he sure has. Never forgets a thing, that one."

"You've been with him a long time, haven't you?"

"Sure . . . since before he found you. I knowed him in Mexico in the war, and that was longer ago than I like to think. I was a boy then, my own self. Son," Roundy said suddenly, "look!"

He tossed a huge pinecone into the air, a big one at least nine inches long.

With a flash of movement, Mike Bastian palmed his gun, and almost as soon as it hit his hand it belched flame—and again. The second shot spattered the cone into a bunch of flying brown chips.

"Not bad!" Roundy nodded. "You still shoot too quick, though. You got to get over that, Mike. Sometimes, one shot is all you'll ever get."

Side-by-side the two walked through the trees, the earth spongy with a thick blanket of pine needles. Roundy was not as tall as Mike, but he walked with the long, springy stride of the woodsman. He smoked in silence for some distance, and then he spoke up.

"Mike, if Ben's ready for you to go out, what will you do?"

For two steps, Bastian said nothing. Then he spoke slowly. "Why, go, I guess. What else?"

"You're sure? You're sure you want to be an outlaw?"

"That's what I was raised for, isn't it?" There was

some bitterness in Mike's voice. "Somebody to take over what Ben Curry started?"

"Yeah, that's what you were raised for, all right. But this you want to remember, Mike. It's your life. Ben Curry, for all his power, can't live it for you. Moreover, times have changed since Ben and me rode into this country. It ain't free and wild like it was, because folks are comin' in, settlin' it up, makin' homes. Gettin' away won't be so easy, and your pards will change, too. In fact, they have already changed. When Ben and me come into this country, it was every man for himself. More than one harum-scarum fella, who was otherwise all right, got himself the name of an outlaw. Nobody figured much about it, then. We rustled cows, but so did half the big ranchers of the West. And if a cowpoke got hard up and stopped a stage, nobody made much fuss unless he killed somebody. They figured it was just high spirits. But the last few years, it ain't like that no more. And it ain't only that the country is growin' up . . . it's partly Ben Curry himself."

"You mean he's grown too big?" Mike put in.

"What else? Why, your dad controls more land than there is in New York State. Got it right under his thumb. And he's feared over half the West by those who knows about him, although not many do.

"Outside of this country around us, nobody ain't seen Ben Curry in years, not leastwise to know him. But they've heard his name, and they know that somewhere an outlaw lives who rules a gang of almost a thousand men. That he robs and rustles where he will, and nobody has nerve enough to chase him.

"He's been smart, just plenty smart," old Roundy went on. "Men ride out and they meet at a given point. The whole job is planned in every detail . . . it's rehearsed, and then they pull it and scatter and meet again here. For a long time folks laid it to driftin' cowpunchers or to gangs passin' through. The way he's set up, one of the gangs he sends out might pull somethin' anywhere from San Antone to Los Angeles, or from Canada to Mexico, although usually he handles it close around.

"He's been the brains, all right, but don't ever forget it was those guns of his that kept things in line. Lately he hasn't used his guns. Kerb Perrin and Rigger Molina or some of their boys handle the discipline. He's become too big, Ben Curry has. He's like a king, and the king isn't gettin' any younger. How do you suppose Perrin will take it when he hears about you takin' over? You think he'll like it?"

"I don't imagine he will," Mike replied thoughtfully. "He's probably done some figuring of his own."

"You bet he has. So has Molina, and neither of them will stop short of murder to get what they want. Your dad still has them buffaloed, I think, but that isn't going to matter when the showdown comes. And I think it's here."

"You do?" Mike said, surprise in his voice.

"Yeah, I sure do. . . ." Roundy hesitated. "You know, Mike, I never told you this, but Ben Curry has a family."

"A *family?*" Despite himself, Mike Bastian was startled.

"Yes, he has a wife and two daughters, and they don't have any idea he's an outlaw. They live down near Tucson somewhere. Occasionally they come to a ranch he owns in Red Wall Cañon, a ranch supposedly owned by Voyle Ragan. He visits them there."

"Does anybody else know this?"

"Not a soul. And don't you be tellin' anybody. You see, Ben always wanted a son, and he never had one. When your real dad was killed down in Mesilla, he took you along with him, and later he told me he was goin' to raise you to take over whatever he left. That was a long time ago, and since then he's spent a sight of time and money on you.

"You can track like an Apache," Roundy said, looking at the tall lad beside him. "In the woods you're a ghost, and I doubt if old Ben Curry himself can throw a gun any faster than you. I'd say you could ride anything that wore hair, and what you don't know about cards, dice, and roulette wheels ain't in it. You can handle a knife and fight with your fists, and you can open anything a man ever made in the way of safes and locks. Along with that, you've had a good education, and you could take care of yourself in any company. I don't reckon there ever was a boy had the kind of education you got, and I think Ben's ready to retire."

"You mean . . . to join his wife and daughters?" Mike questioned.

"That's it. He's gettin' no younger, and he wants it easy-like for the last years. He was always scared of only one thing, and he had a lot of it as a youngster. That's poverty. Well, he's made his pile, and now he wants to step out. Still and all, he knows he can't get out alive unless he leaves somebody behind him that's strong enough and smart enough to keep things under control. That's where you come in."

"Why don't he let Perrin have it?"

"Mike, you know Perrin. He's dangerous, that one. He's poison mean and power crazy. He'd have gone off the deep end a long time ago if it wasn't for Ben Curry. And Rigger Molina is kill crazy. He would have killed fifty men if it hadn't been that he knew Ben Curry would kill him when he got back. No, neither of them could handle this outfit. The whole shebang would go to pieces in ninety days if they had it."

Mike Bastian walked along in silence. There was little that was new in what Roundy was saying, but he was faintly curious as to the old man's purpose. The pair had been much together, and they knew each other as few men ever did. They had gone through storm and hunger and thirst together, living in the desert, mountains, and forest, only rarely returning to the rendezvous in Toadstool Cañon.

Roundy had a purpose in his talking, and Bastian waited, listening. Yet even as he walked, he was conscious of everything that went on around him. A quail had moved back into the tall grass near the stream, and there was a squirrel up ahead in the crotch of a tree. Not far back a gray wolf had crossed the path only minutes ahead of them.

It was as Roundy had said. Mike was a woodsman, and the thought of taking over the outlaw band filled him with unease. Always, he had been aware this time would come, that he had been schooled for it. But before, it had seemed remote and far off. Now, suddenly, it was at hand; it was facing him.

"Mike," Roundy went on, "the country is growin' up. Last spring some of our raids raised merry hell, and some of the boys had a bad time gettin' away. When they start again, there will be trouble and lots of it. Another thing, folks don't look at an outlaw like they used to. He isn't just a wild young cowhand full of liquor, nor a fellow who needs a poke, nor somebody buildin' a spread of his own. Now, he'll be like a wolf, with every man huntin' him. Before you decide to go into this, you think it over, make up your own mind.

"You know Ben Curry, and I know you like him. Well, you should. Nevertheless, Ben had no right to raise you for an outlaw. He went his way of his own free will, and, if he saw it that way, that was his own doin'. But no man has a right to say to another . . . 'This you must do . . . this you must be.' No man has a right to train another, startin' before he has a chance to make up his mind, and school him in any particular way."

The old man stopped to relight his pipe, and

Mike kept a silence, would let Roundy talk out what seemed to bother him.

"I think every man should have the right to decide his own destiny, insofar as he can," Roundy said, continuing his trend of thought. "That goes for you, Mike, and you've got the decision ahead of you. I don't know which you'll do. But if you decide to step out of this gang, then I don't relish bein' around when it happens, for old Ben will be fit to be tied.

"Right now, you're an honest man. You're clean as a whistle. Once you become an outlaw, a lot of things will change. You'll have to kill, too . . . don't forget that. It's one thing to kill in defense of your home, your family, or your country. It's another thing when you kill for money or for power."

"You think I'd have to kill Perrin and Molina?" Mike Bastian asked.

"If they didn't get you first!" Roundy spat. "Don't forget this, Mike, you're fast. You're one of the finest and, aside from Ben Curry, probably the finest shot I ever saw. But that ain't shootin' at a man who's shootin' at you. There's a powerful lot of difference, as you'll see.

"Take Billy the Kid, this Lincoln County gunman we hear about. Frank and George Coe, Dick Brewer, Jesse Evans . . . any one of them can shoot as good as him. The difference is that the part down inside of him where the nerves should be was left out. When he starts shootin' and when he's bein' shot at, he's like ice! Kerb Perrin's that way, too. Perrin's the cold type, steady as a rock. Rigger Molina's another kind of cat . . . he explodes all over the place. He's white-hot, but he's deadly as a rattler."

Mike was listening intently as Roundy continued his description: "Five of them cornered him one time at a stage station out of Julesburg. When the shootin' was over, four of them were down and the fifth was holdin' a gunshot arm. Molina, he rode off under his own power. He's a shaggy wolf, that one. Wild and uncurried and big as a bear."

Far more than Roundy realized did Mike Bastian know the facts about Ben Curry's empire of crime. For three years now, Curry had been leading his foster son through all the intricate maze of his planning. There were spies and agents in nearly every town in the Southwest, and small groups of outlaws quartered here and there on ranches who could be called upon for help at a moment's notice.

Also, there were ranches where fresh horses could be had, and changes of clothing, and where the horses the band had ridden could be lost. At Toadstool Cañon were less than 200 of the total number of outlaws, and many of those, while living under Curry's protection, were not of his band.

Also, the point Roundy raised had been in Mike's mind, festering there, an abscess of doubt and dismay. The Ben Curry he knew was a huge, kindly man, even if grim and forbidding at times. He had taken the homeless boy and given him kindness and care, had, indeed, trained him as a son. Today, however, was the first inkling Mike had of the existence of that other family. Ben Curry had planned and acted with shrewdness and care.

THE TRAIL TO PEACH MEADOW CAÑON

Mike Bastian had a decision to make, a decision that would change his entire life, whether for better or worse.

Here in the country around the Vermilion Cliffs was the only world he knew. Beyond it? Well, he supposed he could punch cows. He was trained to do many things, and probably there were jobs awaiting such a man as himself.

He could become a gambler, but he had seen and known a good many gamblers and did not relish the idea. Somewhere beyond this wilderness was a larger, newer, wealthier land—a land where honest men lived and reared their families.

CHAPTER TWO

In the massive stone house at the head of Toadstool Cañon, so called because of the gigantic toadstool-like stone near the entrance, Ben Curry leaned his great weight back in his chair and stared broodingly out the door over the valley below.

His big face was blunt and unlined as rock, but the shock of hair above his leonine face was turning to gray. He was growing old. Even spring did not bring the old fire to his veins again, and it had been long since he had ridden out on one of the jobs he planned so shrewdly. It was time he quit.

Yet this man, who had made decisions sharply and quickly, was for the first time in his life uncertain. For six years he had ruled supreme in this remote corner north of the Colorado. For twenty years he had been an outlaw, and for fifteen of those twenty years he had ruled a gang that had grown and extended its ramifications until it was an empire in itself.

Six years ago he had moved to this remote country and created the stronghold where he now lived. Across the southern limit rolled the Colorado River, with its long cañons and maze of rocky wilderness, a bar to any pursuit from the country south of the river, where he operated.

As far as other men were concerned, only at Lee's Ferry was there a crossing, and, in a cabin nearby, his men watched it night and day. In fact, there were two more crossings—one that the gang used in going to and from their raids, and the other known only to himself. It was his ace in the hole, even if not his only one.

One law of the gang, never transgressed, was that there was to be no lawless activity in the Mormon country to the north of them. The Mormons and the Indians were left strictly alone and were their friends. So were the few ranchers who lived in the area. These few traded at the stores run by the gang, buying their supplies closer to home and at cheaper prices than they could have managed elsewhere.

Ben Curry had never quite made up his mind about Kerb Perrin. He knew that Perrin was growing restive, that he was aware that Curry was aging and was eager for the power of leadership. Yet the one factor Curry couldn't be certain about was whether Perrin would stand for the taking over of the band by Mike Bastian.

Well, Mike had been well trained; it would be his problem. Ben smiled grimly. He was the old bull of the herd, and Perrin was pawing the dirt, but what would he say when a young bull stepped in? One who had not won his spurs with the gang?

That was why Curry had sent for him, for it was time Mike be groomed for leadership, time he moved out on his first job. And he had just the one. It was big, it was sudden, and it was dramatic. It would have an excellent effect on the gang if it was brought off smoothly, and he was going to let Mike plan the whole job himself.

There was a sharp knock outside, and Curry smiled a little, recognizing it.

"Come in!" he bellowed.

He watched Perrin stride into the room with his quick, nervous steps, his eyes scanning the room.

"Chief," Perrin said, "the boys are gettin' restless. It's spring, you know, and most of them are broke. Have you got anything in mind?"

"Sure, several things. But one that's good and tough. Struck me it might be a good one to break the kid in on."

"Oh?" Perrin's eyes veiled. "You mean he'll go along?"

"No, I'm going to let him run it. The whole show. It will be good for him."

Kerb Perrin absorbed that. For the first time, he felt worry. For the first time, an element of doubt entered his mind. He had wondered before about Bastian and what his part would be in all this.

For years, Perrin had looked forward to the time when he could take over. He knew there would be trouble with Rigger Molina, but he had thought out that phase of it. He knew he could handle it. But what if Curry was planning to jump young Bastian into leadership?

Quick, hot passion surged through Perrin, and,

when he looked up, it was all he could do to keep his voice calm.

"You think that's wise?" he questioned. "How will the boys feel about goin' out with a green kid?"

"He knows what to do," Curry said. "They'll find he's smart as any of them, and he knows plenty. This is a big job, and a tough one."

"Who goes with him?"

"Maybe I'll let him pick them," Curry said thoughtfully. "Good practice for him."

"What's the job?" Perrin asked, voice sullen.

"The gold train."

Perrin's fingers tightened, digging into his palms. This was the job he wanted! The shipment from the mines! It would be enormous, rich beyond anything they had done!

Months before, in talking of this job, he had laid out his plan for it before Curry. But it had been vetoed. He had recommended the killing of every man jack of them, and burial of them all, so the train would vanish completely.

"You sound like Molina," Curry had said, chuckling. "Too bloody."

"Dead men don't talk," he had replied grimly.

Yet, even as he spoke, he was thinking of something else. He was thinking of the effect of this upon the men of the outfit. He knew many of them liked Mike Bastian, and more than one of them had helped train him. In a way, many of the older men were as proud of Mike as if he had been their own son. If he stepped out now and brought off this job, he would acquire power and prestige in the gang equal to Perrin's own.

Fury engulfed Perrin. Curry had no right to do this to him! Sidetracking him for an untried kid. Shoving Bastian down all their throats.

Suddenly the rage died, and in its place came resolution. It was time he acted on his own. He would swing his own job, the one he had had in mind for so long, and that would counteract the effect of the gold-train steal. Moreover, he would be throwing the challenge into Ben Curry's teeth, for he would plan this job without consulting him. If there was going to be a struggle for leadership, it could begin here and now.

"He'll handle the job, all right," Curry said confidently. "He has been trained, and he has the mind for it. He plans well. I hadn't spoken of it before, but I asked his advice on a few things without letting him know why, and he always came through with the right answers."

Kerb Perrin left the stone house filled with burning resentment but also something of triumph. At last, after years of taking orders, he was going on his own. Yet the still, small voice of fear was in him, too. *What would Ben Curry do?*

The thought made him quail. He had seen the cold fury of Curry when it was aroused, and he had seen him use a gun. He himself was fast, but was he as fast as Ben Curry? In his heart, he doubted it. He dismissed the thought, although storing it in his mind. Something would have to be done about Ben Curry. . . .

Mike Bastian stood before Ben Curry's table, and the two men stared at each other.

Ben Curry, the old outlaw chief, was huge, bear-like, and mighty, his eyes fierce yet glowing with a kindly light now, and something of pride, too. Facing him, tall and lithe, his shoulders broad and mighty, was Mike Bastian, child of the frontier, grown to manhood and trained in every art of the wilds, every dishonest practice in the books, every skill with weapons. Yet educated, too, a man who could conduct himself well in any company.

"You take four men and look over the ground yourself, Mike," Ben Curry was saying. "I want you to plan this one. The gold train leaves the mines on the Twentieth. There will be five wagons, the gold distributed among them, although there won't be a lot of it as far as quantity is concerned. That gold train will be worth roughly five hundred thousand dollars.

"When that job is done," he continued, "I'm going to step down and leave you in command. You knew I was planning that. I'm old, and I want to live quietly for a while, and this outfit takes a strong hand to run it. Think you can handle it?"

"I think so," Mike Bastian said softly.

"I think so, too. Watch Perrin . . . he's the snaky one. Rigger is dangerous, but whatever he does will be out in the open. Not so Perrin. He's a conniver. He never got far with me because I was always one jump ahead of him. And I still am."

The old man was silent for a few minutes as he stared out the window.

"Mike," he said then, doubt entering his voice, "maybe I've done wrong. I meant to raise you the way I have. I ain't so sure what is right and wrong, and never was. Never gave it much thought, though.

"When I come West, it was dog eat dog, and your teeth had to be big. I got knocked down and kicked around some, and then I started taking big bites myself. I organized, and then I got bigger. In all these years nobody has ever touched me. If *you've* got a strong hand, you can do the same. Sometimes you'll have to buy men, sometimes you'll have to frighten them, and sometimes you'll have to kill."

He shook his head as if clearing it of memories past, and then glanced up.

"Who will you take with you?" he asked. "I mean, in scouting this layout?"

Ben Curry waited, for it was judgment of men that Bastian would need most. It pleased him that Mike did not hesitate.

"Roundy, Doc Sawyer, Colley, and Garlin."

Curry glanced at him, his eyes hard and curious. "Why?"

"Roundy has an eye for terrain like no man in this world," Mike said. "He says mine's as good, but I'll take him along to verify or correct my judgment. Doc Sawyer is completely honest. If he thinks I'm wrong, he'll say so. As for Colley and Garlin, they are two of the best men in the whole outfit. They will be pleased that I ask their help, which puts them on my side in a measure, and they can see how I work."

Curry nodded. "Smart . . . and you're right. Colley and Garlin are two of the best men, and absolutely fearless." He smiled a little. "If you have trouble with Perrin or Molina, it won't hurt to have them on your side."

Despite himself, Mike Bastian was excited. He was twenty-two years old and by frontier standards had been a man for several years. But in all that time, aside from a few trips into the Mormon country and one to Salt Lake, he had never been out of the maze of cañons and mountains north of the Colorado.

Roundy led the way, for the trail was an old one to him. They were taking the secret route south used by the gang on their raids, and, as they rode toward it, Mike stared at the country. He was always astonished by its ruggedness.

Snow still lay in some of the darker places of the forest, but as they neared the cañon, the high cliffs towered even higher and the trail dipped down through a narrow gorge of rock. Countless centuries of erosion had carved the rock into grotesque figures resembling those of men and animals, colored with shades of brown, pink, gray, and red, and tapering off into a pale yellow. There were shadowed pools among the rocks, some from snow water and others from natural springs, and there were scattered clumps of oak and piñon.

In the bottom of the gorge the sun did not penetrate except at high noon and there the trail wound along between great jumbled heaps of boulders, cracked and broken from their fall off the higher cliffs.

Mike Bastian followed Roundy, who rode hump-shouldered on a ragged, gray horse that seemed as old as he himself but also as sure-footed and mountain-wise. Mike was wearing a black hat now, but his same buckskins. He had substituted boots for the moccasins he usually wore, although they reposed in his saddlebags, ready at hand.

Behind them rode Doc Sawyer, his lean, saturnine face quiet, his eyes faintly curious and interested as he scanned the massive walls of the cañon. Tubby Colley was short and thick-chested, and very confident—a hard-jawed man who had been a first-rate ranch foreman before he shot two men and hit the outlaw trail.

Tex Garlin was tall, rangy, and quiet. He was a Texan, and little else was known of his background, although it was said he could carve a dozen notches on his guns if he had wished.

Suddenly Roundy turned the gray horse and rode abruptly at the face of the cliff, but when he came close up, the sand and boulders broke and a path showed along the under-scoured rock. Following this for several hundred yards, they found a cañon that cut back into the cliff itself and then turned to head toward the river.

The roar of the Colorado, high with spring freshets, was loud in their ears before they reached it. Finally they came out on a sandy bank littered with driftwood.

Nearby was a small cabin and a plot of garden. The door of the house opened, and a tall old man came out.

"Howdy!" he said. "I been expectin' somebody."

His shrewd old eyes glanced from face to face, and then hesitated at sight of Mike. "Ain't seen you before," he said pointedly.

"It's all right, Bill," Roundy said. "This is Mike Bastian."

"Ben Curry's boy?" Bill stared. "I heard a sight of you, son. I sure have! Can you shoot like they say?"

Mike flushed. "I don't know what they say," he said, grinning. "But I'll bet a lot of money I can hit the side of that mountain if it holds still."

Garlin stared at him thoughtfully, and Colley smiled a little.

"Don't take no funnin' from him," Roundy said. "That boy can shoot."

"Let's see some shootin', son," Bill suggested. "I always did like to see a man who could shoot."

Bastian shook his head. "There's no reason for shootin'," he protested. "A man's a fool to shoot unless he's got cause. Ben Curry always told me never to draw a gun unless I meant to use it."

"Go ahead," Colley said. "Show him."

Old Bill pointed. "See that black stick end juttin' up over there? It's about fifty, maybe sixty paces. Can you hit it?"

"You mean that one?" Mike palmed his gun and fired, and the black stick pulverized.

It was a movement so smooth and practiced that no one of the men even guessed he had intended to shoot. Garlin's jaws stopped their calm chewing, and he stared with his mouth open for as long as it took to draw a breath. Then he glanced at Colley.

"Wonder what Kerb would say to that?" he said, astonished. "This kid can shoot."

"Yeah," Colley agreed, "but the stick didn't have a gun."

Old Bill worked the ferry out of a cave under the cliff and freighted them across the swollen river in one hair-raising trip. With the river behind, they wound up through the rocks and started south.

Chapter Three

The mining and cow town of Weaver was backed up near a large hill on the banks of a small creek. Colley and Garlin rode into the place at sundown, and an hour later Doc Sawyer and Roundy rode in.

Garlin and Colley were leaning on the bar having a drink, and they ignored the newcomers. Mike Bastian followed not long afterward and walked to the bar alone.

All the others in the saloon were Mexicans, except for three tough-looking white men lounging against the bar nearby. They glanced at Mike and his buckskins, and one of them whispered something to the others, at which they all laughed.

Doc Sawyer was sitting in a poker game, and his eyes lifted. Mike leaned nonchalantly against the bar, avoiding the stares of the three toughs who stood near him. One of them moved over closer.

"Hi, stranger," he said. "That's a right purty suit you got. Where could I get one like it?"

Garlin looked up and his face stiffened. He

nudged Colley. "Look," Garlin said quickly. "Corbus and Fletcher. An' trouble huntin'. We'd better get into this."

Colley shook his head. "No. Let's see what the kid does."

Mike looked around, his expression mild. "You want a suit like this?" he inquired of the stranger. His eyes were innocent, but he could see the sort of man he had to deal with. These three were toughs, and dangerous. "'Most any Navajo could make one for you."

"Just like that?" Corbus sneered.

He was drinking and in a nagging, quarrelsome mood. Mike looked altogether too neat for his taste.

"Sure. Just like this," Mike agreed. "But I don't know what you'd want with it, though. This suit would be pretty big for you to fill."

"Huh?" Corbus's face flamed. Then his mouth tightened. "You gettin' smart with me, kid?"

"No." Mike Bastian turned, and his voice cracked like a whip in the suddenly silent room. "Neither am I being hurrahed by any lame-brained, liquor-guzzling saddle tramp. You made a remark about my suit, and I answered it. Now, you can have a drink on me, all three of you, and I'm suggesting you drink up." His voice suddenly became soft. "I want you to drink up because I want to be very, very sure we're friends, see?"

Corbus stared at Bastian, a cold hint of danger filtering through the normal stubbornness of his brain. Something told him this was perilous going, yet he was stubborn, too stubborn. He smiled slowly. "Kid," he drawled, "supposin' I don't want to drink with no tenderfoot brat?"

Corbus never saw what happened. His brain warned him as Mike's left hand moved, but he never saw the right. The left stabbed his lips and the right cracked on the angle of his jaw, and he lifted from his feet and hit the floor on his shoulder blades, out cold.

Fletcher and the third tough stared from Corbus to Mike. Bastian was not smiling. "You boys want to drink?" he asked. "Or do we go on from here?"

Fletcher stared at him. "What if a man drawed a gun instead of usin' his fists?" he demanded.

"I'd kill him," Bastian replied quietly.

Fletcher blinked. "I reckon you would," he agreed. He turned and said: "Let's have a drink. That Boot Hill out there's already got twenty graves in it."

Garlin glanced at Colley, his eyebrows lifted. Colley shrugged.

"I wonder what Corbus will do when he gets up?" he said.

Garlin chuckled. "Nothin' today. He won't be feelin' like it."

Colley nodded. "Reckon you're right, an' I reckon the old man raised him a wildcat. I can hardly wait to see Kerb Perrin's face when we tell him."

"You reckon," Garlin asked, "that what we heard is true? That Ben Curry figures to put this youngster into his place when he steps out?"

"Yep, that's the talk," Colley answered.

"Well, maybe he's got it. We'll sure know before this trip is over."

Noise of the stagecoach rolling down the street drifted into the saloon, and Mike Bastian strolled outside and started toward the stage station. The passengers were getting down to stretch their legs and to eat. Three of them were women.

One of them noticed Mike standing there and walked toward him. She was a pale, pretty girl with large gray eyes.

"How much farther to Red Wall Cañon?" she inquired.

Mike Bastian stiffened. "Why, not far. That is, you'll make it by morning if you stick with the stage. There is a cross-country way if you had you a buckboard, though."

"Could you tell us where we could hire one? My mother is not feeling well."

He stepped down off the boardwalk and headed toward the livery stable with her. As they drew alongside the stage, Mike looked up. An older woman and a girl were standing near the stage, but he was scarcely aware of anything but the girl. Her hair was blond, but darker than that of the girl who walked beside him, and her eyes, too, were gray. There the resemblance ended, for where this girl beside him was quiet and sweet, the other was vivid.

She looked at him, and their eyes met. He swept off his hat. The girl beside him spoke.

"This is my mother, Missus Ragan, and my sister Drusilla." She looked up at him quickly. "My name is Juliana."

Mike bowed. He had eyes only for Drusilla, who was staring at him.

"I am Mike Bastian," he said.

"He said he could hire us a rig to drive across country to Red Wall Cañon," Juliana explained. "It will be quicker that way."

"Yes," Mike agreed, "much quicker. I'll see what I can do. Just where in Red Wall did you wish to go?"

"To Voyle Ragan's ranch," Drusilla said. "The V Bar." He had turned away, but he stopped in mid-stride. "Did you say . . . Voyle Ragan's?"

"Yes. Is there anything wrong?" Drusilla stared at him. "What's the matter?"

He regained his composure swiftly. "Nothing. Only, I'd heard the name, and . . ."—he smiled—"I sort of wanted to know for sure, so if I came calling . . ."

Juliana laughed. "Why, of course. We'd be glad to see you."

He walked swiftly away. These, then, were Ben Curry's daughters! That older woman would be his wife! He was their foster brother, yet obviously his name had meant nothing to them. Neither, he reflected, would their names have meant anything to him, nor the destination, had it not been for what Roundy had told him only the previous day.

Drusilla her name was. His heart pounded at the memory of her, and he glanced back through the gathering dusk at the three women standing there by the stage station.

Hiring the rig was a matter of minutes. He liked the look of the driver, a lean man, tall and white-haired. "No danger on that road this time of year," the driver said. "I can have them there in no time by takin' the cañon road."

Drusilla was waiting for him when Mike walked back. "Did you find one?" she asked, and then listened to his explanation and thanked him.

"Would it be all right with you," Mike said, "if I call at the V Bar?"

She looked at him, her face grave, but a dancing light in her eyes. "Why, my sister invited you, did she not?"

"Yes, but I'd like you to invite me, too."

"I?" She studied him for a minute. "Of course, we'd be glad to see you. My mother likes visitors as well as Julie and I, so won't you ask her, too?"

"I'll take the invitation from you and your sister as being enough." He grinned. "If I ask your mother, I might have to ask your father."

"Father isn't with us." She laughed. "We'll see him at Ragan's. He's a rancher somewhere up north in the wilds. His name is Ben Ragan. Have you heard of him?"

"Seems to me I have," he admitted, "but I wouldn't say for sure."

After they had gone, Mike wandered around and stopped in the saloon, after another short talk with a man at the livery stable. Listening and asking an occasional question, he gathered the information he wanted on the gold shipment. Even as he asked the questions, it seemed somehow fantastic that he, of all people, should be planning such a thing.

Never before had he thought of it seriously, but now he did. And it was not only because the thought went against his own grain, but because he was thinking of Drusilla Ragan.

What a girl she was! He sobered suddenly. Yet, for all of that, she was the daughter of an outlaw. Did she know it? From her question, he doubted it very much.

Doc Sawyer cashed in his chips and left the poker game to join Mike at the bar.

"The twentieth, all right," he said softly. "And five of them are going to carry shotguns. There will be twelve guards in all, which looks mighty tough. The big fellow at the poker table is one of the guards, and all of them are picked men."

Staring at his drink, Mike puzzled over his problem. What Roundy had said was of course true. This was a turning point for him. He was still an honest man; yet, when he stepped over the boundary, it would make a difference. It might make a lot of difference to a girl like Dru Ragan, for instance.

The fact that her father, also, was an outlaw would make little difference. Listening to Sawyer made him wonder. Why had such a man, brilliant, intelligent, and well-educated, ever become a criminal?

Sawyer was a gambler and a very skillful one, yet he was a doctor, too, and a fine surgeon. His education was as good as study and money could make it, and it had been under his guidance that Mike Bastian had studied.

"Doc," he said suddenly, "whatever made you ride a crooked trail?"

Sawyer glanced at him suddenly, a new expression in his eyes. "What do you mean, Mike? Do you have doubts?"

"Doubts? That seems to be all I do have these last few days."

"I wondered about that," Doc said. "You have been so quiet that I never doubted but what you were perfectly willing to go on with Ben Curry's plans for you. It means power and money, Mike . . . all a man could want. If it is doubt about the future for outlaws that disturbs you, don't let it. From now on it will be political connections and bribes, but with the money you'll have to work with, that should be easy."

"It should be," Mike said slowly. "Only maybe . . . just maybe . . . I don't want to."

"Conscience rears its ugly head." Sawyer smiled ironically. "Can it be that Ben Curry's instructions have fallen on fallow ground? What started this sudden feeling? The approach of a problem? Fear?" Doc had turned toward Mike and was staring at him with aroused interest. "Or," he added, "is there a woman? A girl?"

"Would that be so strange?"

"Strange? No. I've wondered it hasn't happened before, but then you've lived like a recluse these past years. Who is she?"

"It doesn't matter," Mike answered. "I was thinking of this before I saw her. Wondering what I should do."

"Don't ask me," Sawyer said. "I made a mess of my own life. Partly a woman and partly the desire for what I thought was easy money. Well, there's no such a thing as easy money, but I found that out too late. You make your own decision. What was it Matthew Arnold said? I think you learned the quotation."

" 'No man can save his brother's soul, or pay his brother's debt.' "

"Right. So you save your own and pay your own. There's one thing to remember, Mike. No matter which way you go, there will be killing. If you take over Ben Curry's job, you'll have to kill Perrin and Molina, if you can. And you may have to kill them, and even Ben Curry, if you step out."

"Not Dad," Mike said.

"Don't be so sure. It isn't only what he thinks that matters, Mike. No man is a complete ruler or dictator. His name is only the symbol. He is the mouthpiece for the wishes of his followers, and, as long as he expresses those wishes, he leads them. When he fails, he falls. Ben Curry is the boss not only because he has power in him, but also because he has organization, because he has made them money, because he has offered them safety. If you left, there would be a chink in the armor. No outlaw ever trusts another outlaw who turns honest, for he always fears betrayal."

Bastian tossed off his drink. "Let's check with Roundy. He's been on the prowl."

Roundy came to them hastily. "We've got to get out of town quick," he said. "Ducrow and Fernandez just blew in, and they are drunk and raisin' the devil. Both of them are talkin', too, and, if they see us, they will spill everything."

"All right." Mike straightened. "Get our horses. Get theirs, too. We'll take them with us."

Garlin and Colley had come to the bar. Garlin shook his head. "Ducrow's poison mean when he's drunk, and Fernandez sides with him in everything," Garlin informed. "When Ducrow gets drunk, he always pops off too much. The boss forbade him weeks ago to come down here."

"He's a pal of Perrin's," Colley said, "so he thinks he can get away with it."

"Here they come now!" Roundy exclaimed.

"All right . . . drift," Bastian ordered. "Make it quick with the horses."

Chapter Four

Saloon doors slammed open, and the two men came in. One look, and Mike could see there was cause for worry. Tom Ducrow was drunk and ugly, and behind him was Snake Fernandez. They were an unpleasant pair, and they had made their share of trouble in Ben Curry's organization, although always protected by Perrin.

Bastian started forward, but he had scarcely taken a step when Ducrow saw him.

"There he is!" he bellowed loudly. "The pet! The boss's pet!" He stared around at the people in the barroom. "You know who this man is? He's . . ."

"Ducrow!" Mike snapped. "Shut up and go home. Now!"

"Look who's givin' orders!" Ducrow sneered. "Gettin' big for your britches, ain't you?"

"Your horses will be outside in a minute," Mike said. "Get on them and start back, fast!"

"Suppose," Ducrow sneered, "you make me!"

Mike had been moving toward him, and now with a pantherlike leap he was beside the outlaw and, with a quick slash from his pistol barrel, floored him.

With an oath, Snake Fernandez reached for a gun, and Mike had no choice. He shot him in the shoulder. Fernandez staggered, the gun dropping from his fingers. Mouthing curses, he reached for his left-hand gun.

But even as he reached, Garlin—who had stayed behind when the others went for the horses—stepped up behind him. Jerking the gun from the man's holster, he spun him about and shoved him through the door.

Mike pulled the groggy Ducrow to his feet and pushed him outside after Fernandez.

A big man got up hastily from the back of the room. Mike took one quick glimpse at the star on his chest. "What goes on here?" the sheriff demanded.

"Nothing at all," Mike said affably. "Just a couple of the boys from our ranch feeling their oats a little. We'll take them out and off your hands."

The sheriff stared from Mike to Doc Sawyer and Colley, who had just come through the door.

"Who are you?" he demanded. "I don't believe I know you *hombres*."

"That's right, sir, you don't," Mike said. "We're from the Mogollons, riding back after driving some cattle through to California. It was a rough trip, and this liquor here got to a couple of the boys."

The sheriff hesitated, looking sharply from one to the other.

"*You* may be a cowhand," he said, "but that *hombre*"—he pointed to Sawyer—"looks like a gambler."

Mike chuckled. "That's a joke on you, boy!" he said to Doc. Then he turned back to the sheriff. "He's a doctor, sir, and quite a good one. A friend of my boss's."

A gray-haired man got up and strolled alongside the sheriff. His eyes were alive with suspicion.

"From the Mogollons?" he queried. "That's where I'm from. Who did you say your boss was?"

Doc Sawyer felt his scalp tighten, but Mike smiled.

"Jack McCardle," he said, "of the Flying M. We aren't his regular hands, just a bunch passing through. Doc, here, he being an old friend of Jack's, handled the sale of the beef."

The sheriff looked around.

"That right, Joe?" he asked the gray-haired man. "There's a Flying M over there?"

"Yes, there is." Joe was obviously puzzled. "Good man, too, but I had no idea he was shipping beef."

The sheriff studied Bastian thoughtfully. "Guess you're all right," he said finally. "But you sure don't *talk* like a cowhand."

"As a matter of fact," Mike said, swallowing hard, "I was studying for the ministry, but my interests began to lead me in more profane directions, so I am afraid I backslid. It seems," he said gravely, "that a leaning toward poker isn't conducive to the correct manner in the pulpit."

"I should say not." The sheriff chuckled. "All right, son, you take your pardners with you. Let 'em sleep it off."

Mike turned, and his men followed him. Ducrow and Fernandez had disappeared. They rode swiftly out of town and took the trail for Toadstool Cañon. It wasn't until they were several miles on the road that Sawyer glanced at Mike.

"You'll do," he said. "I was never so sure of a fight in my life."

"That's right, boss," Garlin said. "I was bettin' we'd have to shoot our way out of town. You sure smooth-talked 'em. Never heard it done prettier."

"Sure did," Colley agreed. "I don't envy you havin' Ducrow an' Fernandez for enemies, though."

Kerb Perrin and Rigger Molina were both in conference with Ben Curry when Mike Bastian came up the stone steps and through the door. They both looked up sharply.

"Perrin," Bastian said, "what were Ducrow and Fernandez doing in Weaver?"

"In Weaver?" Perrin straightened up slowly, nettled by Mike's tone, but puzzled, too.

"Yes, in Weaver. We nearly had to shoot our way out of town because of them. They were down there, drunk and talking too much. When I told them to get on their horses and go home, they made trouble."

Kerb Perrin was on dangerous ground. He well

knew how harsh Ben Curry was about talkative outlaws, and, while he had no idea what the two were doing in Weaver, he knew they were trouble-makers. He also knew they were supporters of his. Ben Curry knew it, and so did Rigger Molina.

"They made trouble?" Perrin questioned now. "How?"

"Ducrow started to tell who I was."

"What happened?"

Mike was aware that Ben Curry had tipped back in his chair and was watching him with interest.

"I knocked him down with a pistol barrel," he said.

"You *what?"* Perrin stared. Ducrow was a bad man to tangle with. "What about Fernandez?"

"He tried to draw on me, and I put a bullet in his shoulder."

"You should've killed him," Molina said. "You'll have to, sooner or later."

Kerb Perrin was stumped. He had not expected this, or that Mike Bastian was capable of handling such a situation. He was suddenly aware that Doc Sawyer had come into the room.

Bastian faced Ben Curry. "We got what we went after," he said, "but another bad break like Ducrow and Fernandez, and we'd walk into a trap."

"There won't be another." Curry said harshly.

When Mike had gone out, Doc Sawyer looked at Ben Curry and smiled.

"You should have seen him and heard him," he said as Molina and Perrin were leaving. "It would have done your heart good. He had a run-in with

Corbus and Fletcher, too. Knocked Corbus out with a punch and backed Fletcher down. Oh, he'll do, that boy of yours, he'll do. The way he talked that sheriff out of it was one of the smoothest things I've seen."

Ben Curry nodded with satisfaction. "I knew it. I knew he had it."

Doc Sawyer smiled, and looked up at the chief from under his sunburned eyebrows. "He met a girl, too."

"A girl? Good for him. It's about time."

"This was a very particular girl, chief," Sawyer continued. "I thought you'd like to know. If I'm any judge of men, he fell for her and fell hard. And I'm not so sure it didn't happen both ways. He told me something about it, but I had already seen for myself."

Something in Sawyer's tone made Curry sit up a little. "Who was the girl?" he demanded.

"A girl who came in on the stage." Doc spoke carefully, avoiding Curry's eyes now. "He got the girl and her family a rig to drive them out to a ranch. Out to the V Bar."

Ben Curry's face went white. So Doc knew! It was in every line of him, every tone of his voice. The one thing he had tried to keep secret, the thing known only to himself and Roundy, was known to Doc! And to how many others?

"The girl's name," Doc continued, "was Drusilla Ragan. She's a beautiful girl."

"Well, I won't have it," Curry said in a strained voice.

Doc Sawyer looked up, faintly curious. "You

mean the foster son you raised isn't good enough for your daughter?"

"Don't say that word here!" Curry snapped, his face hard. "Who knows besides you?"

"Nobody of whom I am aware," Doc said with a shrug. "I only know by accident. You will remember the time you were laid up with that bullet wound. You were delirious, and that's why I took care of you myself . . . because you talked too much." Doc lighted his pipe. "They made a nice-looking pair," he said. "And I think she invited him to Red Wall Cañon."

"He won't go! I won't have any of this crowd going there!"

"Chief, that boy's what you made him, but he's not an outlaw yet," Doc said, puffing contentedly on his pipe. "He could be, and he might be, but if he does become one, the crime will lie on your shoulders."

Curry shook himself and stared out the window.

"I said it, chief, the boy has it in him," Sawyer went on. "You should have seen him throw that gun on Fernandez. The kid's fast as lightning. He thinks, too. If he takes over this gang, he'll run this country like you never ran it. I say *if*. . . ."

"He'll do it," Curry said confidently, "you know he will. He always does what I tell him."

Doc chuckled. "He may, and again he may not. Mike Bastian has a mind of his own, and he's doing some thinking. He may decide he doesn't want to take over. What will you do then?"

"Nobody has ever quit this gang. Nobody ever will!"

"You'd order him killed?"

Ben Curry hesitated. This was something he had never dreamed of, something . . . "He'll do what he's told," he repeated, but he was no longer sure.

A tiny voice of doubt was arising within him, a voice that made him remember the Mike Bastian who was a quiet, determined little boy who would not cry, a boy who listened and obeyed. Yet now Curry knew, and admitted it for the first time, that Mike Bastian always had a mind of his own.

Never before had the thought occurred to him that Mike might disobey, that he might refuse. And if he did, what then? It was a rule of the outlaw pack that no man could leave it and live. It was a rule essential to their security. A few had tried, and their bodies now lay in Boot Hill. But Mike, his son? No, not Mike!

Within him, there was a deeper knowledge, an awareness that here his interests and those of the pack would divide. Even if he said no, they would say yes.

"Who would kill him, chief? Kerb Perrin? Rigger Molina? You?" Doc Sawyer shook his head slowly. "You *might* be able to do it, maybe one of the others, but I doubt it. You've created the man who may destroy you, chief, unless you join him."

Long after Doc Sawyer was gone, Ben Curry sat there staring out over the shadowed valley. He was getting old. For the first time he was beginning to doubt his rightness, beginning to wonder if he had not wronged Mike Bastian.

And what of Mike and Dru, his beloved, gray-eyed daughter? The girl with dash and spirit? But why not? Slowly he thought over Mike Bastian's life. Where was the boy wrong? Where was he unfitted for Dru? By the teachings given him by Curry's own suggestion? His own order? Or was there yet time?

Ben Curry heaved himself to his feet and began to pace the carpeted floor. He would have to decide. He would have to make up his mind, for a man's life and future lay in his hands, to make or break.

What if Dru wanted him anyway, outlaw or not? Ben Curry stopped and stared into the fireplace. If it had been Julie now, he might forbid it. But Dru? He chuckled. She would laugh at him. Dru had too much of his own nature, and she had a mind of her own.

Mike Bastian was restless the day after the excitement in Weaver. He rolled out of his bunk and walked out on the terrace. Only he and Doc Sawyer slept in the stone house where Ben Curry lived. Roundy was down in town with the rest of them, but tonight Mike wanted to walk, to think.

There had been a thrill of excitement in outtalking the sheriff, in facing down Fletcher, in flattening Corbus. And there had been more of it in facing Ducrow and Fernandez. Yet, was that what he wanted? Or did he want something more stable, more worthwhile? The something he might find with Drusilla Ragan?

Already he had won a place with the gang. He knew the story would be all over the outlaw camp now.

Walking slowly down the street of the settlement, he turned at right angles and drifted down a side road. He wanted to get away from things for a little while, to think things out. He turned again and stared back into the pines, and then he heard a voice coming from a nearby house. The words halted him.

". . . at Red Wall," Mike heard the ending.

Swiftly he glided to the house and flattened against the side. Kerb Perrin was speaking.

"It's a cinch, and we'll do it on our own without anybody's say-so. There's about two thousand cattle in the herd, and I've got a buyer for them. We can hit the place just about sunup. Right now, they have only four hands on the place, but about the first of next month they will start hiring. It's now or not at all."

"How many men will we take?" That was Ducrow speaking.

"A dozen. That will keep the divvy large enough, and they can swing it. Hell, that Ragan Ranch is easy. The boss won't hear about it until too late, and the chances are he will never guess it was us."

"I wouldn't want him to," Fernandez said.

"To hell with him!" Ducrow was irritated. "I'd like a crack at that Bastian again."

"Stick with me," Perrin said, "and I'll set him up for you. Curry is about to turn things over to him. Well, we'll beat him to it."

"You said there were girls?" Ducrow suggested.

"There's Curry's two girls and a couple of Mexican girls who work there. One older woman. I want one of those girls myself . . . the youngest of the Ragan sisters. What happens to the others is none of my business."

Mike Bastian's hand dropped to his gun, and his lips tightened. The tone of Perrin's voice filled him with fury, and Ducrow was as bad as Perrin.

"What happens if Curry does find out?" Ducrow demanded.

"What would happen?" Perrin said fiercely. "I'll kill him like I've wanted to all these years. I've hated that man like I never hated anyone in my life."

"What about that Bastian?" Ducrow demanded.

Perrin laughed. "That's your problem. If you and Fernandez can't figure to handle him, then I don't know you."

"He knocked out Corbus, too," Ducrow said. "We might get him to throw in with us, if this crowd is all afraid of old Ben Curry."

"I ain't so sure about him my own self," said another voice, which Mike placed as belonging to an outlaw named Bayless. "He may not be so young anymore, but he's hell on wheels with a gun."

"Forget him!" Perrin snapped. Then: "You three, and Clatt, Panelli, Monson, Kiefer and a few others, will go with us. All good men. There's a lot of dissatisfaction, anyway. Molina wants to raid the Mormons. They've a lot of rich stock, and there's no reason why we can't sell it south of the river and the other stock north of it. We can get rich."

Chapter Five

Mike Bastian waited no longer, but eased away from the wall. He was tempted to wait for Perrin and brace him when he came out. His first thought was to go to Ben Curry, but he might betray his interest in Drusilla, and the time was not yet ripe for that. What would her father say if he found the foster son he had raised to be an outlaw was in love with his daughter?

It was foolish to think of it, yet he couldn't help it. There was time between now and the twentieth for him to get back to Red Wall and see her.

A new thought occurred to him. Ben Curry would know the girls and their mother were there and would be going to see them. That would be his chance to learn of Ben's secret pass to the riverbank and how he crossed the Colorado.

Recalling other trips, Bastian knew the route must be a much quicker one than any he knew of, and was probably farther west and south, toward the cañon country. Already he was eager to see the girl again, and all he could think of was her trim figure, the laughter in her eyes, the soft curve of her lips.

There were other things to be considered. If there was as much unrest in the gang as Perrin said, things might be nearing a definite break. Certainly outlaws were not the men to stand hitched for long, and Ben Curry had commanded them for longer than anyone would believe. Their loyalty was due partly to the returns from their ventures under his guidance, and partly to fear of his far-reaching power. But he was growing old, and there were those among them who feared he was losing his grip.

Mike felt a sudden urge to saddle his horse and be gone, to get away from all this potential cruelty, the conniving and hatred that lay dormant here, or was seething and ready to explode. He could ride out now by the Kaibab trail through the forest, skirt the mountains, and find his own way through the cañon. It was a question whether he could escape, whether Ben Curry would let him go. To run now meant to abandon all hope of seeing Dru again, and Mike knew he could not do that.

Returning to his quarters in the big stone house, he stopped in front of a mirror. With deadly, flashing speed, he began to practice quick draws of his guns. Each night he did this twenty times as swiftly as his darting hands could move.

Finally he sat down on his bed thinking. Roundy first, and today Doc Sawyer. Each seemed to be hoping he would throw in the sponge and escape this outlaw life before it was too late. Doc said it was his life, but was it?

There was a light tap on the door. Gun in hand, he reached for the latch. Roundy stepped in. He glanced at the gun.

"Gettin' scary, Mike?" he queried. "Things are happenin'!"

"I know."

Mike went on to explain what he had overheard, and Roundy's face turned serious. "Mike, did you ever hear of Dave Lenaker?"

Bastian looked up. "You mean the Colorado gunman?"

"That's the one. He's headed this way. Ben Curry just got word that Lenaker's on his way to take over the Curry gang!"

"I thought he was one of Curry's ablest lieutenants?"

Roundy shrugged. "He was, Mike, but the word has gone out that the old man is losing his grip, and outlaws are quick to sense a thing like that. Lenaker never had any use for Perrin, and he's most likely afraid that Perrin will climb into the saddle. Dave Lenaker's a holy terror, too."

"Does Dad Curry know?" Mike said.

"Yeah. He's some wrought up, too," Roundy answered. "He was figurin' on bein' away for a few days, one of those trips he takes to Red Wall. Now he can't go."

Morning came cool and clear. Mike Bastian could feel disaster in the air, and he dressed hurriedly and headed for the bunkhouse. Few of the men were eating, and those few were silent. He knew they were all aware of impending change. He was finishing his coffee when Kerb Perrin came in.

Instantly Mike was on guard. Perrin walked with a strut, and his eyes were bright and confident. He glanced at Bastian, faintly amused, and then sat down at the table and began to eat.

Roundy came in, and then Doc Sawyer. Mike dallied over his coffee, and a few minutes later was rewarded by seeing Ducrow come in with Kiefer, followed in a few minutes by Rocky Clatt, Monson, and Panelli.

Suddenly, with the cup half to his mouth, Mike recalled with a shock that this was the group Perrin planned to use on his raid on the Ragan Ranch. That could mean the raid would come off today!

He looked up to see Roundy suddenly push back his chair and leave his breakfast unfinished. The old woodsman hurried outside and vanished.

Mike put down his own cup and got up. Then he stopped, motionless. The hard muzzle of a gun was prodding him in the back, and a voice was saying: "Don't move."

The voice was that of Fernandez, and Mike saw Perrin smiling.

"Sorry to surprise you, Bastian," Perrin said. "But with Lenaker on the road we had to move fast. By the time he gets here, I'll be in the saddle. Some of the boys wanted to kill you, but I figured you'd be a good talkin' point with the old man. He'd be a hard kernel to dig out of that stone shell of his without you. But with you for an argument, he'll come out all right."

"Have you gone crazy, Perrin? You can't get away with this."

"I am, though. You see, Rigger Molina left this morning with ten of his boys to work a little job they heard of. In fact, they are on their way to knock over the gold train."

"The gold train?" Bastian exclaimed. "Why, that was *my* job! He doesn't even know the plan made for it. Or the information I got."

Perrin smiled triumphantly. "I traded with him. I told him to give me a free hand here, and he could have the gold train. I neglected to tell him about the twelve guards riding with it, or the number with shotguns. In fact, I told him only five guards would be along. I think that will take care of Rigger for me." Perrin turned abruptly. "Take his guns and tie his hands behind his back, then shove him out into the street. I want the old man to see him."

"What about *him?*" Kiefer demanded, pointing a gun at Doc Sawyer.

"Leave him alone. We may need a doctor, and he knows where his bread is buttered."

Confused and angry, Mike Bastian was shoved out into the warm morning sun, then jerked around to face up the cañon toward the stone house.

Suddenly fierce triumph came over him. Perrin would have a time getting the old man out of that place. The sunlight was shining down the road from over the house, fully into their faces. The only approach to the house was up thirty steps of stone, overlooked by an upper window of the house. From that window and the doorway, the entire settlement could be commanded by an expert rifleman.

Ben Curry had thought of everything. The front and back doors of every building in the settlement could be commanded easily from his stronghold.

Perrin crouched behind a pile of sandbags hastily thrown up near the door of the store.

"Come on down, Curry!" he shouted. "Give yourself up or we'll kill Bastian!"

There was no answer from up the hill. Mike felt cold and sick in his stomach. Wind touched his hair and blew a strand down over his face. He stared up at the stone house and could see no movement, hear no response.

"Come on out!" Perrin roared again. "We know you're there! Come out or we'll kill your son!"

Still no reply.

"He don't hear you," Clatt said. "Maybe he's still asleep. Let's rush the place."

"You rush it," Kiefer said. "Let me watch!"

Despite his helplessness, Mike felt a sudden glow of satisfaction. Old Ben Curry was a wily fighter. He knew that once he showed himself or spoke, their threat would take force. It was useless to kill Bastian unless they knew Curry was watching them.

Perrin had been so sure Curry would come out rather than sacrifice Mike, and now they were not even sure he was hearing them! Nor, Mike knew suddenly, was anybody sure Ben would come out even if they did warn him Mike would be killed.

"Come on out!" Perrin roared. "Give yourself up and we'll give you and Bastian each a horse and a half mile start! Otherwise, you both die! We've got dynamite!"

Mike chuckled. Dynamite wasn't going to do them much good. There was no way to get close to that stone house, backed up against the mountain as it was.

"Perrin," he said, "you've played the fool. Curry doesn't care whether I live or die. He won't come out of there, and there's no way you can get at him. All he's got to do is sit tight and wait until Dave Lenaker gets here. He will make a deal with Dave then, and where will you be?"

"Shut up!" Perrin bellowed. But for the first time he seemed to be aware that his plan was not working. "He'll come out, all right."

"Let's open fire on the place," Ducrow suggested. "Or rush it like Clatt suggested."

"Hell!" Kiefer was disgusted. "Let's take what we can lay hands on and get out! There's two thousand head of cattle down in those bottoms. Rigger's gone and Lenaker ain't here yet, so let's take what we can an' get out."

"Take pennies when there's millions up there in that stone house?" Perrin demanded. His face swelled in anger and the veins stood out on his forehead. "That strong room has gold in it! Stacks of money! I know it's there. With all that at hand, would you run off with a few cattle?"

Kiefer was silent but unconvinced.

Standing in the dusty street, Mike looked up at the stone house. All the loyalty and love he felt for the old man up there in that house came back with a rush. Whatever he was, good or bad, he owed to Ben Curry. Perhaps Curry had reared him for a life of crime, for outlawry, but to Ben Curry it was not a bad life. He lived like a feudal lord and had respect for no law he did not make himself.

Wrong he might be, but he had given the man that was Mike Bastian a start. Suddenly Mike knew that he could never have been an outlaw, that it was not in him to steal and rob and kill. But that did not mean he could be disloyal to the old man who had reared him and given him a home when he had none.

He was suddenly, fiercely proud of the old man up there alone. Like a cornered grizzly, he would fight to the death. He, Mike Bastian, might die here in the street, but he hoped old Ben Curry would stay in his stone shell and defeat them all.

Kerb Perrin was stumped. He had made his plan quickly when he'd heard Dave Lenaker was on his way here, for he knew that, if Lenaker arrived, it might well turn into a bloody four-cornered fight. But with Molina out of the way, he might take over from Ben Curry before Lenaker arrived, and kill Lenaker and the men he brought with him in an ambush.

He had been sure that Ben Curry would reply, that he might give himself up or at least show himself, and Perrin had a sniper concealed to pick him off if he moved into the open. That he would get nothing but silence, he could not believe.

Mike Bastian stood alone in the center of the street. There was simply nothing he could do. At any moment Perrin might decide to have him killed where he stood. With his hands tied behind him, he was helpless. Mike wondered what had happened to Roundy? The old mountain man had risen suddenly from the table and vanished. Could he be in league with Perrin?

That was impossible. Roundy had always been Ben Curry's friend and had never liked anything about Kerb Perrin.

"All right," Perrin said suddenly, "we'll hold Bastian. He's still a good argument. Some men will stay here, and the rest of us will make that raid on the Ragan outfit. I've an idea that when we come back, Curry will be ready to talk business."

CHAPTER SIX

Bastian was led back from the street and thrown into a room in the rear of the store. There his feet were tied and he was left in darkness.

His mind was in a turmoil. If Perrin's men hit the ranch now, they would take Drusilla and Juliana! He well knew how swiftly they would strike and how helpless any ordinary ranch would be against them. And here he was tied hand and foot, helpless to do anything!

He heaved his body around and fought the ropes that bound him, until sweat streamed from his body. Even then, with his wrists torn by his struggles against the rawhide thongs that made him fast, he did not stop. There was nothing to aid him—no nail, no sharp corner, nothing at all.

The room was built of thin boards nailed to two-by-fours. He rolled himself around until he could get his back against the boards, trying to remember where the nails were. Bracing himself as best he could, he pushed his back against the wall. He bumped against it until his back was sore. But with no effect.

Outside, all was still. Whether they had gone, he did not know. Yet, if Perrin had not gone on his raid, he would be soon leaving. However, if Mike could escape and find Curry's private route across the river, he might beat them to it.

He wondered where Doc Sawyer was. Perhaps he was afraid of what Perrin might do if he tried to help. Where was Roundy?

Just when he had all but given up, he had an idea—a solution so simple that he cursed himself for not thinking of it before. Mike rolled over and got up on his knees and reached back with his bound hands for his spurs. Fortunately he was wearing boots instead of the moccasins he wore in the woods. By wedging one spur against the other, he succeeded in holding the rowel almost immovable, and then he began to chafe the rawhide with the prongs of the rowel.

Desperately he sawed, until every muscle was crying for relief. As he stopped, he heard the rattle of horses' hoofs. They were just going! Then he had a fighting chance if he could get free and get his hands on a gun!

He knew he was making headway, for he could feel the notch he had already cut in the rawhide. Suddenly footsteps sounded outside. Fearful whoever was there would guess what he was doing, Mike rolled over on his side.

The door opened and Snake Fernandez came in, and in his hand he held a knife. His shoulder was bandaged crudely but tightly, and the knife was held in his left hand. He came in and closed the door.

Mike stared, horror mounting within him. Perrin was gone, and Snake Fernandez was moving toward him, smiling wickedly.

"You think you shoot Pablo Fernandez, eh?" the outlaw said, leering. "Now, we see who shoots. I am going to cut you to little pieces. I am going to cut you very slowly."

Bastian lay on his shoulder and stared at Fernandez. There was murder in the outlaw's eyes, and all the savagery in him was coming to the fore. The man stooped over him and pricked him with the knife. Clamping his jaws, Mike held himself tense.

Rage mounted in the man. He leaned closer. "You do not jump, eh? I make you jump."

He stabbed down hard with the knife, and Mike whipped over on his shoulder blades and kicked out wickedly with his bound feet. The movement caught the killer by surprise. Mike's feet hit him in the knees and knocked him rolling. With a lunge, Mike rolled over and jerked at the ropes that bound him.

Something snapped, and he jerked again. Like a cat, the killer was on his feet now, circling warily. Desperately Mike pulled at the ropes, turning on his shoulders to keep his feet toward Fernandez. Suddenly he rolled over and hurled himself at the Mexican's legs, but Fernandez jerked back and stabbed.

Mike felt a sliver of pain run along his arms, and then he rolled to his feet and jerked wildly at the thongs. His hands came loose suddenly and he hurled himself at Fernandez's legs, grabbing one ankle.

Fernandez came down hard, and Bastian jerked at the leg, and then scrambled to get at him. One hand grasped the man's wrist, the other his throat. With all the power that was in him, Mike shut down on both hands.

Fernandez fought like an injured wildcat, but Mike's strength was too great. Gripping the throat with his left hand, Mike slammed the Mexican's head against the floor again and again, his throttling grip freezing tighter and tighter.

The outlaw's face went dark with blood, and his struggles grew weaker. Mike let go of his throat hold suddenly and slugged him three times on the chin with his fist.

Jerking the knife from the unconscious man's hand, Mike slashed at the thongs that bound his ankles. He got to his feet shakily. Glancing down at the sprawled-out Fernandez, he hesitated. The man was not wearing a gun, but must have had one. It could be outside the door. Easing to the door, Mike opened it a crack.

The street was deserted as far as he could see. His hands felt awkward from their long constraint, and he worked his fingers to loosen them up. There was no gun in sight, so he pushed the door wider. Fernandez's gun belts hung over the chair on the end of the porch.

He had taken two steps toward them when a man stepped out of the bunkhouse. The fellow had a toothpick lifted to his lips, but when he saw Mike

Bastian, he let out a yelp of surprise and went for his gun.

It was scarcely fifteen paces and Mike threw the knife underhanded, pitching it point first off the palm of his hand. It flashed in the sun as the fellow's gun came up. Then Mike could see the haft protruding from the man's middle section.

The fellow screamed and, dropping the gun, clutched at the knife hilt in an agony of fear. His breath came in horrid gasps that Mike could hear as he grabbed Fernandez's guns and belted them on. Then he lunged for the mess hall, where his own guns had been taken from him. Shoving open the door, he sprang inside, gun in hand.

Then he froze. Doc Sawyer was standing there smiling, and Doc had a shotgun on four of Perrin's men. He looked up with relief.

"I was hoping you would escape," he said. "I didn't want to kill these men and didn't know how to go about tying them up by myself."

Mike caught up his own guns, removed Fernandez's gun belts, and strapped on his own. Then he shoved the outlaw's guns inside the waistband of his pants.

"Down on the floor," he ordered. "I'll tie them, and fast."

It was the work of only a few minutes to have the four outlaws bound hand and foot. He gathered up their guns. "Where's Roundy?" he asked.

"I haven't seen him since he left here," Doc said. "I've been wondering."

"Let's go up to the house. We'll get Ben Curry,

and then we'll have things under control in a hurry."

Together, they went out the back door and walked swiftly down the line of buildings. Mike took off his hat and sailed it into the brush, knowing he could be seen from the stone house and hoping that Ben Curry would recognize him. Sawyer was excited, but trying to appear calm. He had been a gambler and, while handy with guns, was not a man accustomed to violence. Always before, he had been a bystander rather than an active participant.

Side-by-side, gambling against a shot from someone below, they went up the stone stairs.

There was no sound from within the house. They walked into the wide living room and glanced around. There was no sign of anyone. Then Mike saw a broken box of rifle shells.

"He's been around here," he said. Then he looked up and shouted: "Dad!"

A muffled cry reached them, and Mike was out of the room and up another staircase. He entered the room at the top, and then froze in his tracks. Sawyer was behind him now.

This was the fortress room, a heavy-walled stone room that had water trickling from a spring in the wall of the cliff and running down a stone trough and out through a pipe. There was food stored here, and plenty of ammunition.

The door was heavy and could be locked and barred from within. The walls of this room were all of four feet thick, and nothing short of dynamite could have blasted a way in.

This was Ben Curry's last resort, and he was here now. But he was sprawled on the floor, his face contorted with pain.

"Broke my leg," he panted. "Too heavy. Tried to move too . . . fast. Slipped on the steps, dragged myself up here." He looked up at Mike. "Good for you, Son! I was afraid they had killed you. You got away by yourself?"

"Yes, Dad."

Sawyer had dropped to his knees, and now he looked up.

"This is a bad break, Mike," he said. "He won't be able to move."

"Get me on a bed where I can see out of that window." Ben Curry's strength seemed to flow back with his son's presence. "I'll stand them off. You and me, Mike, we can do it!"

"Dad," Mike said. "I can't stay. I've got to go."

Ben Curry's face went gray with shock, then slowly the blood flowed back into it. Bastian dropped down beside him.

"Dad, I know where Perrin's going. He's gone to make a raid on the Ragan Ranch. He wants the cattle and the women."

The old man lunged so mightily that Sawyer cried out and tried to push him back. Before he could speak, Mike said: "Dad, you must tell me about the secret crossing of the Colorado that you know. I must beat them to the ranch."

Ben Curry's expression changed to one of vast relief and then quick calculation. He nodded.

"You could do it, but it'll take tall riding." Quickly he outlined the route, and then added:

"Now, listen! At the river there's an old Navajo. He keeps some horses for me, and he has six of the finest animals ever bred. You cross that river and get a horse from him. He knows about you."

Mike got up. "Make him comfortable, Doc. Do all you can."

Sawyer stared at Mike. "What about Dave Lenaker? He'll kill us all!"

"I'll take care of Lenaker!" Curry flared. "I'm not dead by a danged sight. I'll show that renegade where he heads in. The moment he comes up that street, I'm going to kill him." He looked at Mike again. "Son, maybe I've done wrong to raise you like I have, but if you kill Kerb Perrin or Lenaker, you would be doing the West a favor. If I don't get Dave Lenaker, you may have to. So remember this, *watch his left hand!*"

Mike ran down the steps and stopped in his room to grab his .44 Winchester. It was the work of a minute to throw a saddle on a horse, and then he hit the trail. Ben Curry and Doc Sawyer could, if necessary, last for days in the fortress-like room—unless, somehow, dynamite was pitched into the window. He would have to get to the Ragan Ranch and then get back here as soon as possible.

Mike Bastian left the stable and wheeled the gray he was riding into the long, winding trail through the stands of ponderosa and fir. The horse was in fine fettle and ready for the trail, and he let it out. His mind was leaping over the trail, turning each bend, trying to see how it must lay.

This was all new country to him, for he was

heading southwest now into the wild, unknown region toward the great cañons of the Colorado, a region he had never traversed and, except for old Ben Curry, was perhaps never crossed by any except Indians.

How hard the trail would be on the horse, Mike could not guess, but he knew he must ride fast and keep going. His route was the shorter, but Kerb Perrin had a lead on him and would be hurrying to make his strike and return.

Patches of snow still hid themselves around the roots of the brush and in the hollows under the end of some giant deadfall. The air was crisp and chill, but growing warmer, and by afternoon it would be hot in the sunlight. The wind of riding whipped his black hair. He ran the horse down a long path bedded deep with pine needles, and then turned at a blazed tree and went out across the arid top of a plateau.

This was the strange land he loved, the fiery, heat-blasted land of the sun. Riding along the crest of a long ridge, he looked out over a long valley dotted with mesquite and sagebrush. Black dots of cattle grazing offered the only life beyond the lonely, lazy swing of a high-soaring buzzard.

He saw the white rock he had been told to look for and turned the free-running horse into a cleft that led downward. They moved slowly here, for it was a steep slide down the side of the mesa and out on the long roll of the hill above the valley.

Time and time again Mike's hand patted his guns, as if to reassure himself they were there. His thoughts leaped ahead, trying to foresee what would happen. Would he arrive only to find the buildings burned and the girls gone?

He knew only that he must get there first, that he must face them, and that at all costs he must kill Kerb Perrin and Ducrow. Without them, the others might run, might not choose to fight it out. Mike had an idea that without Perrin, they would scatter to the four winds.

Swinging along the hillside, he took a trail that led again to a plateau top and ran off through the sage, heading for the smoky-blue distance of the cañon.

Chapter Seven

Mike's mind lost track of time and distance, leaping ahead to the river and the crossing, and beyond it to Ragan's V Bar Ranch. Down steep trails through the great, broken cliffs heaped high with the piled-up stone of ages, and down through the wild, weird jumble of boulders, and across the flat top lands that smelled of sage and piñon, he kept the horse moving.

Then he was once more in the forests of the Kaibab. The dark pines closed around him, and he rode on in the vast stillness of virgin timber, the miles falling behind, the trail growing dim before him.

Then suddenly the forest split aside and he was on the rim of the cañon—an awful blue immensity yawning before him that made him draw the gray to a halt in gasping wonder. Far out over that vast, misty blue rose islands of red sandstone, islands that were laced and crossed by bands of purple and yellow. The sunset was gleaming on the vast plateaus and buttes and peaks with a ruddy glow, fading into opaqueness in the deeper cañon.

The gray was beaten and weary now. Mike turned the horse toward a break in the plateau and rode down it, giving the animal its head. They came out upon a narrow trail that hung above a vast gorge, its bottom lost in the darkness of gathering dusk. The gray stumbled on, seeming to know its day was almost done.

Dozing in the saddle, almost two hours later Mike Bastian felt the horse come to a halt. He jerked his head up and opened his eyes. He could feel the dampness of a deep cañon and could hear the thundering roar of the mighty river as it charged through the rock-walled slit. In front of him was a square of light.

"Halloo, the house!" he called.

He swung down as the door opened.

"Who's there?" a voice cried out.

"Mike Bastian!" he said, moving toward the house with long, swinging strides. "For Ben Curry!"

The man backed into the house. He was an ancient Navajo, but his eyes were keen and sharp.

"I want a horse," Mike said.

"You can't cross the river tonight." The Navajo spoke English well. "It is impossible."

"There'll be a moon later," Mike answered. "When it comes up, I'm going across."

The Indian looked at him, and then shrugged.

"Eat," he said. "You'll need it."

"There are horses?"

"Horses?" The Navajo chuckled. "The best a

man ever saw. Do you suppose Ben Curry would have horses here that were not the best? But they are on the other side of the stream, and safe enough. My brother is with them."

Mike fell into a seat. "Take care of my horse, will you? I've most killed him."

When the Indian was gone, Mike slumped over on the table, burying his head in his arms. In a moment he was asleep, dreaming wild dreams of a mad race over a strange misty-blue land with great crimson islands, riding a splendid black horse and carrying a girl in his arms. He awakened with a start. The old Indian was sitting by the fireplace, and he looked up.

"You'd better eat," he said. "The moon is rising."

They went out together, walking down the path to the water's edge. As the moon shone down into the cañon, Mike stared at the tumbling stream in consternation. Nothing living could swim in that water! It would be impossible.

"How do you cross?" he demanded. "No horse could swim that. And a boat wouldn't get fifty feet before it would be dashed to pieces."

The Indian chuckled. "That isn't the way we cross it. You are right in saying no boat could cross here, for there is no landing over there, and the cañon is so narrow that the water piles up back of the narrows and comes down with a great rush."

Mike looked at him again. "You talk like an educated man," he said. "I don't understand."

The Navajo shrugged. "I was for ten years with a missionary, and after I traveled with him as an interpreter he took me back to the States, where I stayed with him for two years. Then I lived in Sante Fé."

He was leading the way up a steep path that skirted the cliff but was wide enough to walk comfortably. Opposite them, the rock wall of the cañon lifted and the waters of the tumbling river roared down through the narrow chasm.

"Ben Curry does things well, as you shall see," the guide said. "It took him two years of effort to get this bridge built."

Mike stared. "Across there?"

"Yes. A bridge for a man with courage. It is a rope bridge, made fast to iron rings sunk in the rock."

Mike Bastian walked on the rocky ledge at the edge of the trail and looked out across the gorge. In the pale moonlight he could see two slim threads trailing across the cañon high above the tumbling water. Just two ropes, and one of them four feet above the other.

"You mean," he said, "that Ben Curry crossed on *that?*"

"He did. I have seen him cross that bridge a dozen times, at least."

"Have you crossed it?"

The Navajo shrugged. "Why should I? The other side is the same as this, is it not? There is nothing over there that I want."

Mike looked at the slender strands, and then he took hold of the upper rope and tentatively put a foot on the lower one. Slowly, carefully he eased out above the raging waters.

One slip and he would be gone, for no man

could hope to live in those angry flood waters. He slid his foot along, then the other, advancing his handholds as he moved. Little by little, he worked his way across the cañon.

He was trembling when he got his feet in the rocky cavern on the opposite side and so relieved to be safely across that he scarcely was aware of the old Indian who sat there awaiting him.

The Navajo got up and without a word started down the trail. He quickly led Mike to a cabin built in the opening of a dry, branch cañon, and tethered before the door of the cabin was a huge bay stallion.

Waving at the Indian, Mike swung into the saddle, and the bay turned, taking to the trail as if eager to be off.

Would Perrin travel at night? Mike doubted it, but it was possible, so he kept moving himself. The trail led steadily upward, winding finally out of the cañon to the plateau.

The bay stallion seemed to know the trail; it was probable that Curry had used this horse himself. It was a splendid animal, big and very fast. Letting the horse have his head, Mike felt the animal gather his legs under him. Then he broke into a long, swinging lope that literally ate up the ground. How long the horse could hold that speed he did not know, but it was a good start.

It was at least a ten-hour ride to the Ragan V Bar Ranch.

The country was rugged and wild. Several times, startled deer broke and ran before him, and there were many rabbits. Dawn was breaking faintly in the east now, and shortly after daybreak he stopped near a pool of melted snow water and made coffee. Then he remounted the rested stallion and raced on.

Drusilla Ragan brushed her hair thoughtfully, and then pinned it up. Outside, she could hear her mother moving about and the Mexican girls who helped around the house whenever they were visiting. Julie was up, she knew, and had been up for hours. She was outside, talking to that blond cowhand from New Mexico, the one Voyle Ragan had hired to break horses.

Suddenly she heard Julie's footsteps, and then the door opened.

"Aren't you ready yet?" Julie asked. "I'm famished!"

"I'll be along in a minute." Then as Julie turned to go: "What did you think of him, Julie . . . that cowboy who got the buckboard for us? Wasn't he the handsomest thing?"

"Oh, you mean that Mike Bastian?" Julie said. "I was wondering why you were mooning around in here. Usually you're the first one up. Yes, I expect he is good-looking. But did you see the way he looked when you mentioned Uncle Voyle? He acted so strange."

"I wonder if Uncle Voyle knows anything about him? Let's ask!"

"You ask," Julie replied, laughing. "He's *your* problem!"

Voyle Ragan was a tall man, but lean and without Ben Curry's weight. He was already seated at the table when they came in, and Dru was no sooner in her seat than she put her question. Voyle's face became a mask.

"Mike Bastian?" he said thoughtfully. "I don't know. Where'd you meet him?"

The girls explained, and he nodded.

"In Weaver?" Voyle Ragan knew about the gold train, and his eyes narrowed. "I think I know who he is, but I never saw him that I heard of. You probably won't see him again, because most of those riders from up in the strip stay there most of time. They are a wild bunch."

"On the way down here," Julie said, "the man who drove was telling us that outlaws live up there."

"Could be. It's wild enough." Voyle Ragan lifted his head, listening. For a moment he had believed he heard horses. But it was too soon for Ben to be coming. If anyone else came, he would have to get rid of them, and quickly.

He heard the sound again, and then he saw the cavalcade of horsemen riding into the yard. Voyle came to his feet abruptly.

"Stay here!" he snapped.

His immediate thought was of a posse, and then he saw Kerb Perrin. He had seen Perrin many times, although Perrin had never met him. Slowly he moved up to the door, uncertain of his course. These were Ben's men, but Ben had always told him that none of them was aware that he owned this ranch or that Voyle was his brother.

"Howdy!" Voyle said. "What can I do for you?"

Kerb Perrin swung down from his horse. Behind him Monson, Ducrow, and Kiefer were getting down.

"You can make as little trouble as you know how," Perrin said, his eyes gleaming. "All you got to do is stay out of the way. Where's the girls? We want them, and we want your cattle."

"What is this?" Voyle demanded. He wasn't wearing a gun; it was hanging from a clothestree in the next room. "You men can't get away with anything here!"

Perrin's face was ugly as he strode toward the door. "That's what *you* think," he sneered.

The tall old man blocked his way, and Perrin shoved him aside. Perrin had seen the startled faces of the girls inside and knew the men behind him were spreading out.

Ragan swung suddenly, and his fist struck Perrin in the mouth. The gunman staggered, and his face went white with fury.

A Mexican started from the corral toward the house, and Ducrow wheeled, firing from the hip. The man cried out and sprawled over on the hard-packed earth, moaning out his agony.

Perrin had drawn back slowly, his face ugly with rage, a slow trickling of blood from his lips. "For that, I'll kill you!" he snarled at Ragan.

"Not yet, Perrin!"

The voice had a cold ring of challenge, and Kerb Perrin went numb with shock. He turned slowly, to see Mike Bastian standing at the corner of the corral.

CHAPTER EIGHT

Kerb Perrin was profoundly shocked. He had left Bastian a prisoner at Toadstool Cañon. Since he was free now, it could mean that Ben Curry was back in the saddle. It could mean a lot of things. An idea came with startling clarity to him. He had to kill Mike Bastian, and kill him now!

"You men have made fools of yourselves!" Bastian's voice was harsh. He stood there in his gray buckskins, his feet a little apart, his black hair rippled by the wind. "Ben Curry's not through! And this place is under his protection. He sent me to stop you, and stop you I shall! Now, any of you who don't want to fight Ben Curry, get out while the getting is good!"

"Stay where you are!" Perrin snapped. "I'll settle with you, Bastian . . . right now!"

His hand darted down in the sweeping, lightning-fast draw for which he was noted. His lips curled in sneering contempt. Yet, as his gun lifted, he saw flame blossom from a gun in Bastian's hand, and a hard object slugged him. Perplexed and disturbed, he took a step backward. Whatever had hit him had knocked his gun out of line. He turned it toward Bastian again. The gun in Mike's hand blasted a second time, and a third.

Perrin could not seem to get his own gun leveled. His mind wouldn't function right, and he felt a strangeness in his stomach, his legs—suddenly he was on his knees. He tried to get up and saw a dark pool forming near his knees. He must have slipped, he must have—that was blood.

It was his blood!

From far off he heard shouts, then a scream, then the pound of horses' hoofs. Then the thunder of those hoofs seemed to sweep through his brain and he was lying face down in the dirt. And then he knew. Mike Bastian had beaten him to the draw. Mike Bastian had shot him three times. Mike Bastian had killed him!

He started to scream a protest—and then he just lay there on his face, his cheek against the bloody ground, his mouth half open.

Kerb Perrin was dead.

In the instant that Perrin had reached for his gun, Ducrow had suddenly cut and run toward the corner of the house. Kiefer, seeing his leader gunned down, then made a wild grab for his own weapon. The old man in the doorway killed him with a hastily caught up rifle.

The others broke for their horses. Mike rushed after them and got off one more shot as they raced out of the yard. It was then he heard the scream, and whirled.

Ducrow had acted with suddenness. He had come to the ranch for women, and women he intended to have. Even as Bastian was killing Perrin, he had rushed for the house. Darting around the corner where two saddle horses were waiting, he was just in time to see Juliana, horrified at the killing, run back into her bedroom. The bedroom window opened beside Ducrow, and the outlaw reached through and grabbed her.

Julie went numb with horror. Ducrow threw her across Perrin's saddle, and with a pigging string, which he always carried from his days as a cowhand, he jerked her ankles together under the horse's belly.

Instantly he was astride the other horse. Julie screamed then. Wheeling, he struck her across the mouth with a backhand blow. He caught up the bridle of her horse and drove in spurs to his own mount, and they went out of the ranch yard at a dead run.

Mike hesitated only an instant when he heard Julie scream, and then ran for the corner of the house. By the time he rounded the corner, gun in hand, the two horses were streaking into the piñons. In the dust, he could only catch a glimpse of the riders. He turned and walked back.

That had been a woman's scream, but Dru was in the doorway and he had seen her. Only then did he recall Julie. He sprinted for the doorway.

"Where's Julie?" he shouted to Drusilla. "Look through the house!"

He glanced around quickly. Kerb Perrin, mouth agape, lay dead on the hard earth of the ranch yard. Kiefer lay near the body of the Mexican Ducrow had killed. The whole raid had been a matter of no more than two or three minutes.

Voyle Ragan dashed from the house. "Julie's gone!" he yelled hoarsely. "I'll get a horse!"

Bastian caught his arm. His own dark face was tense and his eyes wide.

"You'll stay here!" he said harshly. "Take care of the women and the ranch. I'll go after Julie."

Dru ran from the house. "She's gone, Mike, she's gone! They have her!"

Mike walked rapidly to his horse, thumbing shells into his gun. Dru Ragan started to mount another horse. "You go back to the house," he ordered.

Dru's chin came up. In that moment she reminded him of Ben Curry.

"She's my sister!" Dru cried. "When we find her, she may need a woman's care!"

"All right," Mike said, "but you'll have to do some riding."

He wheeled the big bay around. The horse Dru had mounted was one of Ben Curry's beautiful horses, bred not only for speed but for staying power.

Mike's mind leaped ahead. Would Ducrow get back with the rest of them? Would he join Monson and Clatt? If he did, it was going to be a problem. Ducrow was a handy man with a six-gun, and tackling the three of them, or more if they were all together, would be nothing less than suicide.

He held the bay horse's pace down. He had taken a swift glance at the hoof marks of the horses he was trailing and knew them both.

Would Ducrow head back for Toadstool Cañon? Bastian considered that as he rode, and decided he would not. Ducrow did not know that Julie was Ben Curry's daughter. But from what Mike had said, Ducrow had cause to believe that Ben was back in the saddle again. And men who went off on rebel raids were not lightly handled by Curry. Besides, he would want, if possible, to keep the girl for himself.

Mike had been taught by Roundy that there was more to trailing a man than following his tracks, for you trailed him down the devious paths of the mind as well. He tried to put himself in Ducrow's place.

The man could not have much food, yet on his many outlaw forays he must have learned the country and would know where there was water. Also, there were many ranch hang-outs of the outlaws that Ducrow would know. He would probably go to one of them. Remembering the maps that Ben Curry had shown him and made him study, Mike knew the locations of all those places.

The trail turned suddenly off through the chaparral, and Mike turned to follow. Drusilla had said nothing since they started. Once he glanced at her. Even now, with her face dusty and tear-streaked, she was lovely. Her eyes were fastened on the trail, and he noted with a little thrill of satisfaction that she had brought her rifle along.

Dru certainly was her father's daughter, and a fit companion for any man.

Bastian turned his attention back to the trail. Despite the small lead he had, Ducrow had vanished. That taught Mike something of the nature of the man he was tracing; his years of outlawry had taught him how to disappear when need be. The method was simple. Turning off into the thicker desert growth, he had ridden down into a sandy wash.

Here, because of the deep sand and the tracks of horses and cattle, tracking was a problem and it took Mike several minutes to decide whether Ducrow had gone up or down the wash. Then he caught a hoof print and they were off, winding up the sandy wash. Yet Mike knew they would not be in that sand for long. Ducrow would wish to save his horses' strength.

True enough, the trail soon turned out. From then on, it was a nightmare. Ducrow ran off in a straightaway, and then turned at right angles, weaving about in the sandy desert. Several times he had stopped to brush out portions of his trail, but Roundy had not spent years training Mike Bastian in vain. He hung to the trail like a bloodhound.

Dru, riding behind him, saw him get off and walk, saw him pick up sign where she could see nothing.

Hours passed, and the day slowly drew toward an end. Dru, her face pale, realized night would come before they found her sister. She was about to speak, when Mike looked at her.

"You wanted to come," he said, "so you'll have to take the consequences. I'm not stopping because of darkness."

"How can you trail them?"

"I can't." He shrugged. "But I think I know where they are going. We'll take a chance."

Darkness closed around them. Mike's shirt stuck to his body with sweat, and a chill wind off the higher plateaus blew down through the trees. He rode on, his face grim and his body weary with long hours in the saddle. The big bay kept on, seemingly unhurt by the long hours of riding. Time and again he patted the big horse, and Dru could hear him talking to it in a low voice. Suddenly at the edge of a clearing, he reined in.

"Dru," he said, "there's a ranch ahead. It's an outlaw hang-out. There may be one or more men there. Ducrow may be there. I am going up to find out."

"I'll come, too," the girl said impulsively.

"You'll stay here." His voice was flat. "When I whistle, then you come. Bring my horse along."

He swung down and, slipping off his boots, pulled on his moccasins. Then he went forward into the darkness. Alone, she watched him vanish toward the dark bulk of the buildings. Suddenly a light came on—too soon for him to have arrived.

Mike weaved his way through sage and mesquite to the corral and worked his way along the bars. Horses were there, but it was too dark to make them out. One of them stood near, and he put his hand through the bars, touching the horse's flank. It was damp with sweat.

His face tightened.

The horse stepped away, snorting. As if waiting for just that sound, a light went on in the house; a lamp had been lighted. By that time Mike was at the side of the house, flattened against the wall, peering in.

He saw a heavy, square-faced man with a pistol in his hand. The man put the gun under a towel on the table, and then began pacing around the room, waiting. Mike smiled grimly, walked around the house, and stepped up on the porch. In his moccasins, he made no sound. He opened the door suddenly and stepped into the room.

Chapter Nine

Obviously the man had been waiting for the sound of boots or horses, or the jingle of spurs. Even a knock. Mike Bastian's sudden appearance startled him, and he straightened up from the table, his hand near the towel that covered the gun.

Bastian closed the door behind him. The man stared at the black-haired young man who faced him, stared with puckered brow. This man didn't look like a sheriff to him. Not those tied-down guns or that gray buckskin stained with travel, and no hat.

"You're Walt Sutton," Mike snapped. "Get your hands off that table before I blow you wide open. Get 'em off!"

He drew his gun and jammed the muzzle into Sutton's stomach with such force that it doubled the man up.

Then he swept the towel from the gun on the table.

"You fool!" he said sharply. "If you'd tried that, I'd have killed you!"

Sutton staggered back, his face gray. He had never even seen Mike's hand move.

"Who are you?" he gasped, struggling to get his wind back.

"I'm Mike Bastian, Ben Curry's foster son. He owns this ranch. He set you up here and gave you stock to get started with. Now you double-cross him! Where's Ducrow?"

Sutton swallowed. "I ain't seen him!" he protested.

"You're a liar, Sutton. His horses are out in that corral. I could pistol-whip you, but I'm not going to. You're going to tell me where he is, and now . . . or I'm going to start shooting!"

Walt Sutton was unhappy. He knew Ducrow as one of Ben Curry's men who had come here before for fresh horses. He had never seen this man who called himself Mike Bastian, yet, so far as he knew, no one but Curry himself had ever known the true facts about his ranch. If this man was lying, how could he know?

"Listen, mister," he protested, "I don't want no trouble . . . least of all with old Ben. He did set me up here. Sure, I seen Ducrow, but he told me the law was after him."

"Do I look like the law?" Mike snapped. "He's kidnapped the daughter of a friend of Curry's, niece of Voyle Ragan. I've got to find him."

"Kidnapped Voyle's niece? Gosh, mister, I wondered why he wanted two saddle horses."

Mike whistled sharply. "Where'd he go?" he demanded then.

"Damned if I know," Sutton answered. "He come in here maybe an hour ago, wanted two saddle horses and a pack horse loaded with grub. He took two canteens then and lit out."

Drusilla appeared now in the doorway, and Walt Sutton's eyes went to her.

"I know you," he said. "You're one of Voyle Ragan's nieces."

"She is," Mike said. "Ducrow kidnapped the other one. I'm going to find him. Get us some grub, but fast!"

Mike paced restlessly while Sutton filled a pack and strapped it behind the saddle of one of the fresh horses he furnished them. The horses were some of those left at the ranch by Ben Curry's orders and were good.

"No pack horses," Mike had said. "We're traveling fast." Now, he turned to Sutton again. "You got any idea where Ducrow might be going?"

"Well"—Sutton licked his lips—"he'd kill me if he knowed I said anything, but he did say something about Peach Meadow Cañon."

"Peach Meadow?" Bastian stared at Sutton. The cañon was almost a legend in the Coconino country. "What did he ask you?"

"If I knowed the trail in there, an' if it was passable."

"What did you say?"

Sutton shrugged. "Well, I've heard tell of that there cañon ever since I been in this country, an' ain't seen no part of it. I've looked, all right. Who wouldn't look, if all they say is true?"

When they were about to mount their horses, Mike turned to the girl and put his hand on her arm.

"Dru," he said, "it's going to be rough, so if you want to go back, say so."

"I wouldn't think of it," she said firmly.

"Well, I won't say I'm sorry, because I'm not. I'll sure like having you beside me. In fact"—he hesitated, and then went on—"it will be nice having you."

That was not what he had started to say, and Dru knew it. She looked at Mike for a moment, her eyes soft. He was tired now, and she could see how drawn his face was. She knew only a little of the ride he had made to reach them before Perrin's outlaws came.

When they were in the saddle, Mike explained a little of what he had in mind. "I doubt Ducrow will stop for anything now," he said. "There isn't a good hiding place within miles, so he'll head right for the cañon country. He may actually know something about Peach Meadow Cañon. If he does, he knows a perfect hideaway. Outlaws often stumble across places in their getaways that a man couldn't find if he looked for it in years."

"What is Peach Meadow Cañon?" Dru asked.

"It's supposed to be over near the river in one of the deep cañons that branch off from the Colorado. According to the story, a fellow found the place years ago, but the Spanish had been there before him, and the Indians before them. There are said to be old Indian ruins in the place, but no way to get into it from the plateau. The Indians found a way through some caves in the Coconino sandstone, and the Spanish are supposed to have reached it by boat.

"Anyway," he continued, "this prospector who found it said the climate was tropical, or almost. That it was in a branch cañon, that there was fresh water and a nice meadow. Somebody had planted some fruit trees, and, when he went back, he took a lot of peach pits and was supposed to have planted an orchard.

"Nobody ever saw him or it again," Mike went on, "so the place exists only on his say-so. The Indians alive now swear they never heard of it. Ducrow might be trying to throw us off, or he might honestly know something."

For several miles the trail was a simple thing. They were riding down the floor of a high-walled cañon from which there was no escape. Nevertheless, from time to time Bastian stopped and examined the sandy floor with matches. Always the tracks were there and going straight down the cañon.

This was new country to Mike. He knew the altitude was gradually lessening and believed they would soon emerge on the desert plateau that ran toward the cañon and finally lost itself on the edge of the pine forest.

When they had traveled about seven miles, the cañon ended abruptly and they emerged in a long valley. Mike reined in and swung down.

"Like it or not," he said, "here's where we stop. We can't have a fire, because from here it could be seen for miles. We don't want Ducrow to believe we stopped."

Mike spread his poncho on the sand and handed Dru a blanket. She was feeling the chill and gathered it closely around her.

"Aren't you cold?" she said suddenly. "If we sat close together, we could share the blanket."

He hesitated, and then sat down alongside her and pulled the blanket across his shoulders, grateful for the warmth. Leaning back against the rock, warmed by their proximity and the blanket, they dozed a little.

Mike had loosened the girths and ground-hitched the horses. He wasn't worried about them straying off.

When the sky was just faintly gray, he opened his eyes. Dru's head was on his shoulder and she was sleeping. He could feel the rise and fall of her breathing against his body. He glanced down at her face, amazed that this could happen to him—that he, Mike Bastian, foster son of an outlaw, could be sitting alone in the desert, with this girl sleeping on his shoulder.

Some movement of his must have awakened her, for her breath caught, and then she looked up. He could see the sleepy smile in her eyes and on her mouth.

"I was tired." She whispered the words and made no effort to move her head from his shoulder. "You've nice shoulders," she said. "If we were riding anywhere else, I'd not want to move at all."

"Nor I." He glanced at the stars. "We'd better get

up. I think we can chance a very small fire and a quick cup of coffee."

While he was breaking dried mesquite and greasewood, Dru got the pack open and dug out the coffee and some bread. There was no time for anything else.

The fire made but little light, shielded by the rocks and kept very small, and there was less glow now because of the grayness of the sky. They ate quickly.

When they were in the saddle again, he turned down the trail left by the two saddle horses and the pack horse he was following. Sign was dim, but could be followed without dismounting. Dawn broke, and the sky turned red and gold, then blue. The sun lifted and began to take some of the chill from their muscles.

The trail crossed the valley, skirting an alkali lake, and then dipped into the rocky wilderness that preceded the pine forest. He could find no signs of a camp. Julie, who lacked the fire and also the strength of Dru, must be almost dead with weariness, for Ducrow was not stopping. Certainly the man had more than a possible destination before him. In fact, the farther they rode, the more confident Mike was that the outlaw knew exactly where he was headed.

The pines closed around them, and the trail became more difficult to follow. It was slow going, and much of it Mike Bastian walked. Suddenly he stopped, scowling.

The trail, faint as it had been, had vanished into thin air!

"Stay where you are," he told Dru. "I've got to look around a bit."

Mike studied the ground carefully. Then he walked back to the last tracks he had seen. Their own tracks did not cover them, as he had avoided riding over them in case he needed to examine the hoof prints once more.

Slowly Mike paced back and forth over the pine needles. Then he stopped and studied the surrounding timber very carefully. It seemed to be absolutely uniform in appearance. Avoiding the trail ahead, he left the girl and circled into the woods, describing a slow circle around the horses.

There were no tracks.

He stopped, his brow furrowed. It was impossible to lose them after following so far—yet they were gone, and they had left no trail. He walked back to the horses again, and Dru stared at him, her eyes wide.

"Wait a minute," he said as she began to speak. "I want to think."

He studied, inch by inch, the woods on his left, the trail ahead, and then the trail on his right. Nothing offered a clue. The tracks of three horses had simply vanished as though the animals and their riders had been swallowed into space.

On the left the pines stood thick, and back inside the woods the brush was so dense as to allow no means of passing through it. That was out, then. He had studied that brush and had walked through those woods, and, if a horseman did turn that way there would be no place to go.

The trail ahead was trackless, so it had to be on

the right. Mike turned and walked again to the woods on his right. He inched over the ground, yet there was nothing, no track, no indication that anything heavier than a rabbit had passed that way. It was impossible, yet it had happened.

"Could they have backtracked?" Dru asked suddenly. "Over their same trail?"

Mike shook his head. "There were no tracks," he said, "but those going ahead, I think. . . ." He stopped dead still, and then swore. "I'm a fool! A darned fool!" He grinned at her. "Lend me your hat."

Puzzled, she removed her sombrero and handed it to him. He turned and, using the hat for a fan, began to wave it over the ground to let the wind disturb the surface needles. Patiently he worked over the area around the last tracks seen, and then to the woods on both sides of the trail. Suddenly he stopped.

"Got it," he said. "Here they are."

Dru ran to him. He pointed to a track, then several more.

"Ducrow was smart," Mike explained. "He turned at right angles and rode across the open space, and then turned back down the way he had come, riding over on the far side. Then he dismounted and, coming back, gathered pine needles from somewhere back in the brush and came along here, pressing the earth down and scattering the needles to make it seem there had been no tracks at all."

Mounting again, they started back, and from time to time he dismounted to examine the trail.

Suddenly the tracks turned off into thick woods. Leading their horses, they followed.

"Move as quietly as you can," Mike said softly. "We may be close now. Or he may wait and try to ambush us."

"You think he knows we're following him?" Dru asked.

"Sure. And he knows I'm a tracker. He'll use every trick in the book now."

For a while, the trail was not difficult to follow, and they rode again. Mike Bastian could not take his mind from the girl who rode with him. What would she think when she discovered her father was an outlaw—that he was the mysterious leader of the outlaws?

Chapter Ten

Pine trees thinned out, and before them was the vast blue and misty distance of the cañon. Mike slid to the ground and walked slowly forward on moccasined feet. There were a few scattered pines and the cracked and splintered rim of the cañon, breaking sharply off to fall away into the vast depths. Carefully he scouted the edge of the cañon, and, when he saw the trail, he stopped, flat-footed, and stared, his heart in his mouth.

Had they gone down *there?* He knelt on the rock. Yes, there was the scar of a horse's hoof. He walked out a little farther, looking down.

The cliff fell away for hundreds of feet without even a hump in the wall. Then, just a little farther along, he saw the trail. It was a rocky ledge scarcely three feet wide that ran steeply down the side of the rock from the cañon's rim. On the left the wall, on the right the vast, astonishing emptiness of the cañon.

Thoughtfully he walked back and explained.

"All right, Mike." Dru nodded. "If you're ready, I am.

He hesitated to bring the horses, but decided it would be the best thing. He drew his rifle from the saddle scabbard and jacked a shell into the chamber.

Dru looked at him, steady-eyed. "Mike, maybe he'll be waiting for us," she said. "We may get shot. Especially you."

Bastian nodded. "That could be," he agreed.

She came toward him. "Mike, who are you? What are you? Uncle Voyle seemed to know you, or about you, and that outlaw, Perrin. He knew you. Then I heard you say Ben Curry had sent you to stop them from raiding the ranch. Are you an outlaw, Mike?"

For as long as a man might have counted a slow ten, Mike stared out over the cañon, trying to make up his mind. Now, at this stage, there was only one thing he could say.

"No, Dru, not exactly, but I was raised by an outlaw," he explained. "Ben Curry brought me up like his own son, with the idea that I would take over the gang when he stepped out."

"You lived with them in their hide-out?"

"When I wasn't out in the woods." He nodded. "Ben Curry had me taught everything . . . how to shoot, to track, to ride, even to open safes and locks."

"What's he like, this Ben Curry?" Dru asked.

"He's quite a man," Mike Bastian said, smiling. "When he started outlawing, everybody was rustling a few cows, and he just went a step further and robbed banks and stages, or planned the robberies and directed them. I don't expect he really figured himself bad. He might have done a lot of other things, for he has brains. But he killed a man . . . and then, in getting away, he killed another. The first one was justified. The second one . . . well, he was in a hurry."

"Are you apologizing for him?" Dru said quickly. "After all, he was an outlaw and a killer."

He glanced at her. "He was, yes. And I am not making any apologies for him, nor would he want them. He's a man who always stood on his own two feet. Maybe he was wrong but there were the circumstances. And he was mighty good to me. I didn't have a home, no place to go, and he took me in and treated me right."

"Was he a big man, Mike? A big old man?"

He did not look her way. She knew, then?

"In many ways," he said, "he is one of the biggest men I know. We'd better get started."

It was like stepping off into space, yet the horses took it calmly enough. They were mountain bred and would go anywhere as long as they could get a foothold on something.

The red maw of the cañon gaped to receive them, and they went down, following the narrow, switchback trail that seemed to be leading them into the very center of the earth.

It was late afternoon before they started down, and now the shadows began to creep up the cañon walls, reaching with ghostly fingers for the vanished sunlight. Overhead the red blazed with the setting sun's reflection and seemed to be hurling arrows of flame back into the sky. The depths of the cañon seemed chill after the sun on the plateau, and Mike walked warily, always a little ahead of the horse he was leading.

Dru was riding, and, when he glanced back once, she smiled brightly at him, keeping her eyes averted from the awful depths below.

Mike had no flair for making love, for his knowledge of women was slight. He wished now that he knew more of their ways, knew the things to say that would appeal to a girl.

A long time later they reached the bottom, and far away on their right they could hear the river rushing through the cañon. Mike knelt, and, striking a match, he studied the trail. The tracks turned back into a long cañon that led back from the river.

He got into the saddle then, his rifle across his saddle, and rode forward.

At the end, it was simple. The long chase had led to a quiet meadow, and he could smell the grass before he reached it, could hear the babble of a small stream. The cañon walls flared wide, and he saw, not far away, the faint sparkle of a fire.

Dru came alongside him. "Is . . . that them?" she asked, low-voiced.

"It couldn't be anyone else." Her hand was on his arm and he put his own hand over it. "I've got to go up there alone, Dru. I'll have to kill him, you know."

"Yes," she said simply, "but don't *you* be killed." He started to ride forward, and she caught his arm. "Mike, why have you done all this?" she asked. "She isn't your sister."

"No." He looked very serious in the vague light. "She's yours."

He turned his head and spoke to the horse. The animal started forward.

When, shortly, he stopped the mount, he heard a sound nearby. Dru Ragan was close behind him.

"Dru," he whispered, "you've *got* to stay back. Hold my horse. I'm going up on foot."

He left her like that and walked steadily forward. Even before he got to the fire, he could see them. The girl, her head slumped over on her arms, half dead with weariness, and Ducrow, bending over the fire. From time to time Ducrow glanced at the girl. Finally he reached over and cuffed her on the head.

"Come on, get some of this coffee into you," he growled. "This is where we stay . . . in Peach Meadow Cañon. Might as well give up seein' that sister of yours, because you're my woman now." He sneered. "Monson and them, they ran like scared foxes. No bottom to them. I come for a woman, and I got one."

"Why don't you let me go?" Juliana protested. "My father will pay you well. He has lots of money."

"Your pa?" Ducrow stared at her. "I thought Voyle Ragan was your uncle?"

"He is. I mean Ben Ragan. He ranches up north of the cañon."

"North of the cañon?" Ducrow laughed. "Not unless he's a Mormon, he don't. What's he look like, this pa of yours?"

"He's a great big man, with iron-gray hair, a

heavy jaw. . . ." She stopped, staring at Ducrow. "What's the matter with you?"

Ducrow got slowly to his feet. "Your pa . . . Ben Ragan? A big man with gray hair, an' maybe a scar on his jaw . . . that him?"

"Oh, yes. Take me to him. He'll pay you well."

Suddenly Ducrow let out a guffaw of laughter. He slapped his leg and bellowed. "Man, oh, man! Is that a good one! You're Ben Curry's daughter! Why, that old . . ." He sobered. "What did you call him? Ragan? Why, honey, that old man of yours is the biggest outlaw in the world. Or was until today. Well, of all the . . ."

"You've laughed enough, Ducrow!"

As Mike Bastian spoke, he stepped to the edge of the firelight.

"You leave a tough trail, but I followed it."

Ducrow turned, half crouching, his cruel eyes glaring at Bastian.

"Roundy was right," he snarled. "You could track a snake across a flat rock! Well, now that you're here, what are you goin' to do?"

"That depends on you, Ducrow. You can drop your guns, and I'll take you in for a trial. Or you can shoot it out."

"Drop my guns?" Ducrow chuckled. "You'd actually take me in, too! You're too soft, Bastian. You'd never make the boss man old Ben Curry was. He would never even've said yes or no. He would have seen me and gone to blastin'! You got a sight to learn, youngster. Too bad you ain't goin' to live long enough to learn it."

Ducrow lifted one hand carelessly and wiped it

across the tobacco-stained stubble of his beard. His right hand swept down for his gun even as his left touched his face. His gun came up, spouting flame.

Mike Bastian palmed his gun and momentarily held it rigid. Then he fired.

Ducrow winced like he had been slugged in the chest, and then he lifted on his tiptoes. His gun came level again. "You're . . . fast," he gasped. "Devilish fast."

He fired, and then Mike triggered his gun once more. The second shot spun Ducrow around and he fell, face down, at the edge of the fire.

Dru came running, her rifle in her hand, but when she saw Mike still standing, she dropped the rifle and ran to him. "Oh, Mike!" she sobbed. "I was so frightened! I thought you were killed!"

Julie started to rise, and then fell headlong in a faint. Dru rushed to her side.

Mike Bastian absently thumbed shells into his gun and stared down at the fallen man. He had killed a third man. Suddenly, and profoundly, he wished with all his heart he would never have to kill another.

He holstered his weapon and, gathering up the dead man, carried him away from the fire. He would bury him here, in Peach Meadow Cañon.

CHAPTER ELEVEN

Sunlight lay upon the empty street of the settlement in Toadstool Cañon when Mike Bastian, his rifle crosswise on his saddle, rode slowly into the lower end of the town.

Beside him, sitting straight in her saddle, rode Dru Ragan. Julie had stayed at the ranch, but Dru had flatly refused. Ben Curry was her father, and she was going to him, outlaw camp or not.

If Dave Lenaker had arrived, Mike thought, he was quiet enough, for there was no sound. No horses stood at the hitch rails, and the doors of the saloon were wide open.

Something fluttered on the ground, and Mike looked at it quickly. It was a torn bit of cloth on a man's body. The man was a stranger. Dru noticed it and her face paled.

His rifle at ready, Mike rode on, eyes shifting from side to side. A man's wrist lay in sight across a windowsill, his pistol on the porch outside. There was blood on the stoop of another house.

"There's been a fight," Mike said, "and a bad one. You'd better get set for the worst."

Dru said nothing, but her mouth held firm. At the last building, the mess hall, a man lay dead in a doorway. They rode on, and then drew up at the foot of the stone steps, and dismounted. Mike shoved his rifle back in the saddle scabbard and loosened his six-guns.

"Let's go," he said.

The wide verandah was empty and still, but when he stepped into the huge living room, he stopped in amazement. Five men sat about a table playing cards.

Ben Curry's head came up and he waved at them. "Come on in, Mike!" he called. "Who's that with you? Dru, by all that's holy!"

Doc Sawyer, Roundy, Garlin, and Colley were there. Garlin's head was bandaged, and Colley had one foot stretched out, stiff and straight, as did Ben Curry. But all were smiling.

Dru ran to her father and fell on her knees beside him.

"Oh, Dad!" she cried. "We were so scared!"

"What happened here?" Mike demanded. "Don't sit there grinning! Did Dave Lenaker come?"

"He sure did, and what do you think?" Doc said. "It was Rigger Molina got him! Rigger got to Weaver and found out Perrin had double-crossed him before he ever pulled the job. He discovered that Perrin had lied about the guards, so he rushed back. When he found out that Ben was crippled and that Kerb Perrin had run out, he waited for Lenaker himself.

"He was wonderful, Mike," Doc continued. "I never saw anything like it! He paced the verandah out there like a bear in a cage, swearing and waiting for Lenaker. Muttered . . . 'Leave you in the lurch, will they? I'll show 'em! Lenaker thinks he can gun you down because you're gettin' old, does he? Well, killer I may be, but I can kill him!' And he did, Mike. They shot it out in the street down there. Dave Lenaker, as slim and tall as you, and that great bear of a Molina.

"Lenaker beat him to the draw," Doc went on. "He got two bullets into the Rigger, but Molina wouldn't go down. He stood there, spraddle-legged, in the street and shot until both guns were empty. Lenaker kept shooting and must have hit Molina five times, but when he went down, Rigger walked over to him and spat in his face. 'That's for double-crossers!' he said. He was magnificent!"

"They fooled me, Mike," Roundy said. "I seen trouble a-comin' an' figured I'd better get to old Ben. I never figured they'd slip in behind you like they done. Then the news of Lenaker comin' got me. I knowed him an' was afraid of him, so I figured in order to save Ben Curry I'd get down the road and dry-gulch him. Never killed a gunslinger like him in my life, Mike, but I was sure aimin' to. But he got by me on another trail. After Molina killed Lenaker, his boys and some of them from here started after the gold they'd figured was in this house."

"Doc here," Garlin said, "is some fighter. I didn't know he had it in him."

"Roundy, Doc, Garlin, an' me," Colley said, "we sided Ben Curry. It was a swell scrap while it lasted. Garlin got one through his scalp, and I got two bullets in the leg. Aside from that, we came out all right."

Briefly, then, Mike explained all that had transpired, how he had killed Perrin, and then had trailed Ducrow to Peach Meadow Cañon and the fight there.

"Where's the gang?" he demanded now. "All gone?"

"All the live ones." Ben Curry nodded grimly. "There's a few won't go anywhere. Funny, the only man who ever fooled me was Rigger Molina. I never knew the man was that loyal, yet he stood by me when I was in no shape to fight Lenaker. Took that fight right off my hands. He soaked up lead like a sponge soaks water."

Ben Curry looked quickly at Dru. "So you know you're the daughter of an outlaw? Well, I'm sorry, Dru. I never aimed for you to know. I was gettin' shet of this business and planned to settle down on a ranch with your mother and live out the rest of my days plumb peaceful."

"Why don't you?" Dru demanded.

He looked at her, his admiring eyes taking in her slim, well-rounded figure. "You reckon she'll have me?" he asked. "She looked a sight like you when she was younger, Dru."

"Of course, she'll have you. She doesn't know . . . or didn't know until Julie told her. But I think she guessed. I knew. I saw you talking with some men once, and later heard they were outlaws, and then I began hearing about Ben Curry."

Curry looked thoughtfully from Dru to Mike.

"Is there something between you two? Or am I an old fool?"

Mike flushed and kept his eyes away from Dru.

"He's a fine man, Dru," Doc Sawyer said. "And well educated, if I do say so . . . who taught him all he knows."

"All he knows!" Roundy stared at Doc with contempt. "Book larnin'! Where would that gal be but for what I told him? How to read sign, how to foller a trail? Where would she be?"

Mike took Dru out to the verandah then.

"I can read sign, all right," he said, "but I'm no hand at reading the trail to a woman's heart. You would have to help me, Dru."

She laughed softly, and her eyes were bright as she slipped her arm through his. "Why, Mike, you've been blazing a trail over and back and up again, ever since I met you in the street at Weaver." Suddenly she sobered. "Mike, let's get some cattle and go back to Peach Meadow Cañon. You said you could make a better trail in, and it would be a wonderful place. Just you and I and . . ."

"Sure," he said. "In Peach Meadow Cañon."

Roundy craned his head toward the door, and then he chuckled.

"That youngster," he said. "He may not know all the trails, but he sure gets where he's goin'. He sure does!"

SHOWDOWN TRAIL

Chapter One

With slow, ponderously rhythmical steps, the oxen moved, each step a pause and an effort, each movement a deadening drag. Fine white dust hung in a sifting cloud above the wagon train, caking the nostrils of animals and men, blanketing the lean sides of oxen and horses, dusting with a thin film the clothing of men and women.

Red-rimmed and bloodshot eyes stared with dazed weariness into the limitless distance before them, seeing nothing, knowing nothing. Long since all had been forgotten but heat, dust, and aching muscles. Each succeeding step lifted a powdery dust, stifling and irritating. It lay a foot deep on the endless plain, drowning the sparse grass and sage.

Rock Bannon, riding away from the train and alone, drew in his steel-dust stallion and turned in the saddle, looking back over the covered wagons, sixteen of them in a long line with some lead horses and a few outriders, yet not one who rode so far out as himself.

From where he sat he could not see their faces, but in the days just past he had seen them many times, and the expression of each was engraved in his mind. Haggard, worn, hungry for rest and cool water, he knew that in the secret heart of each was a longing to stop.

The vision was in them yet, the golden promise of the distant hills, offering a land of milk and honey, the fair and flowering land sought by all wandering peoples of whatever time and whatever place. No hardship could seem too great, no trail too long, no mountains impassable when the vision was upon them.

It was always and forever the same when men saw the future opening beyond the hills where the sun slept. Yet this time the vision must hold meaning, this time the end of the trail must bring realization, for they had brought their women and children along.

All had done so but Rock Bannon. He had neither woman nor child, or anyone, anywhere. He had a horse and a saddle, a ready gun, and a mind filled with lore of the trail, and eyes ever fixed on something he wanted, something faint and indistinct in outline, ever distant, yet ever real.

Only of late, as he rode alone on the far flank of the wagon train, had that something begun to take shape and outline, and the shape was that of Sharon Crockett. His somber green eyes slanted back now to the last wagon but one, where the red-gold hair of Sharon on the driver's seat was a flame no dust could dim. In the back of that heavily loaded wagon was Tom Crockett, her father, stirring, restless with fever, and hurt, nursing a bullet wound in his thigh, a memento of the battle with Buffalo Hide's warriors.

From the head of the train came a long, melodious halloo, and Cap Mulholland swung his arm in a great circle, and the lead oxen turned ponderously to swing in the beginning of the circle. Rock touched the gray with his heels and rode slowly toward the wagon train. He was never sure these days as to his reception.

Cap's beard was white with dust as he looked up. Weariness and worry showed in his face. "Rock," he said, "we could sure use a little fresh meat. We're all a mite short on rations, and you seem to be the best hunter amongst us."

"All right," Rock said, "I'll see what I can do after I get Crockett's wagon in place."

Mulholland's head turned sharply. "Bannon, I'd let that girl alone if I were you. No offense intended, but she ain't your kind. I ain't denyin' you've been a sight of help to us. In fact, I don't know what we'd have done without you, and we're glad you came along, but Sharon Crockett's another story. Her pa's bedded down now, and in no shape to speak."

Bannon turned the steel-dust sharply. His face was grim and his jaw hard. "Did he ask you to speak to me? Or did she?"

"Well, no . . . not exactly," Mulholland said uncomfortably. "But I'm headin' this train."

"Then I'll thank you to mind your own business.

Headin' this wagon train is job enough for any man. Any time the Crocketts ask me to stay away, I'll stay, but that's their affair."

Mulholland's face flushed and his eyes darkened with anger. "She ain't your kind," he persisted, "you bein' a killer and all."

Rock Bannon stared at him. "You didn't seem to mind my killing Indians," he said sarcastically. "In fact, you killed a few yourself."

"Don't get me wrong," Cap persisted. "I ain't gainsayin' you ain't helped us. Without you I don't know if we could have beat off those Indians or not, but killin' Indians and killin' our own kind is a lot different thing!"

"You're new to the West, Cap." Bannon's voice was rough. "In a short time you'll find there's men out here that need killin' a sight worse than Indians. In fact, I'm not so sure those Indians jumped us without help."

"What do you mean?" Mulholland demanded.

"I mean," Bannon said, "that Morton Harper told you there'd be no hostile Indians on this route. I warned you of Buffalo Hide then, but he told you he ranged farther north. You took his advice on this trail, not mine."

Pagones and Pike Purcell were coming up to join them. Pike heard the last remark, and his lean, lantern-jawed face flushed with anger.

"You ridin' Harper again?" he harshly demanded of Bannon. "He said this was a better trail, and it is. We ain't had no high passes, and we had six days of the best travel we've had since we left Council Bluffs, with plenty of water and plenty of grass. Now we get a few bad days and a brush with Indians, but that ain't much." He glared at Rock. "I'm sick of your whinin' about this trail and Harper! I figure he's a durned good man. He was sure a help to me when I needed it. Out of supplies, no medicine for the wife, and he staked me."

"I wasn't talking to you," Rock replied shortly, "and I don't like your tone. As far as your loan from Harper, remember that you haven't heard from him on it yet. I've a hunch he'll collect, and plenty."

"I don't need no killer to tell me my business!" Pike snapped, reining his horse around to face Rock. "And I ain't afeerd of no reputation for killin', neither. You don't bluff me none."

"Here, here!" Cap protested. "We can't afford to have trouble in camp. You'll have to admit, Pike, that we'd have been in bad shape a couple of times in that fight if it hadn't been for Bannon. He's been a help. I don't agree with him on Mort Harper, either, but every man to his own idea."

Rock swung the steel-dust and cantered off toward the hills. Inwardly he was seething. He was a fool to stay on with the wagon train—he understood that perfectly well. Not a man here liked him; not a man here talked to him except on business. He was not even a member of their train except by accident.

They had found him at the crossing of the Platte. Riding, half dead, with two bullet wounds in his body, his horse ready to drop with fatigue, he had run up to the wagon train. Sharon Crockett had bedded him down in her wagon and cared for him, and he had ridden on in the same place where her father rode now.

He had offered no explanation of his wounds, had talked but little. A grim and lonely man, gentle words came hard, and he could only look up into Sharon's face and wonder at her beauty, tongue-tied and helpless. Yet his hard, tough, trail-battered body was too used to pain to remain helpless for long. He had recovered rapidly, and afterward he had ridden along with the wagons, hunting for fresh meat and helping when he could.

He was not a man who made friends easily, yet gradually the ice was melting, and the clannishness of the wagon train was breaking down. Twice he had even talked with Sharon, riding beside her wagon, speaking of the mountains and his own wild and lonely life. All that had ended abruptly that night beside the campfire at the fort.

They had been seated around the fire eating supper, listening to the bustle of life around the fort, when a tall, handsome man rode up on a beautiful black mare. Perfectly groomed, his wide, white hat topping coal-black hair that hung to his shoulders, a drooping black mustache and a black broadcloth suit, the trousers tucked into hand-tooled boots, Morton Harper had been a picture to take any eye.

Swinging down, he had walked up to the fire. "Howdy, folks!" His voice was genial, his manner warm and pleasant. In an instant his personality and voice had done what Rock Bannon's could not do in two weeks. He had broken down their reserve and become one of the group. "Headin' for California?"

"Reckon we are," Mulholland had agreed. "We ain't rightly decided whether to stay on the Humboldt Trail or to swing north and go to Oregon."

"Why go either way?" Harper asked. "There's a southern route I could recommend that would be much easier going for your womenfolks." His alert eyes had already found and appraised Sharon Crockett. "More water, plenty of grass, and no high mountain passes."

Cap Mulholland looked up interestedly. "We ain't heard of no such pass, nor no such trail," he admitted. "How does she go?"

"Man named Hastings scouted some of it, and I scouted the rest myself. It is a more southerly route, and within another few months all the travel will be going that way. Right now"—he winked—"the trains that go that way are going to have a mighty fine trip of it. Very little dust except in one stretch, fine grass, lots of water. Also, the hostile Indians are all raiding far north of there along the traveled routes.

"But," he added, "I can see you're well led, and you'll no doubt learn about this trail yourselves. From the look of your teams I'd say you were lucky in your choice of a leader."

Leaning against the hub of a wagon wheel, Rock Bannon ate in silence. The even, smooth flow of the stranger's language had an enchanting quality, but his own hard-grained, cynical character was impervious to mere talk.

As the hours flowed by, Harper sat among them, pleasing the men with subtle flattery, the women with smiles. The reserve of the group thawed under his easy manner, and before long they began to discuss his trail and its possibilities, considering themselves fortunate to know of it first.

There was some talk of putting it to a vote, but it was morning before it came to that. Until then, Rock was silent. "You'd do better," he interposed suddenly, "to stick to the regular trail."

Harper's head came up sharply, and his eyes leveled at Bannon. "Have you ever been over the trail I suggest, my friend?"

"Part way," Rock replied. "Only part of it."

"And was that part easy going for oxen and horses? Was there a good trail? Grass? Water?"

"Yes, I reckon it has all that, but I wouldn't advise it."

"You say it is a better trail but you wouldn't advise it?" Harper glanced around at the others, smiling tolerantly. "That doesn't make much sense, does it? I've been over the entire trail and found it very good going. Moreover, I can give you a map of the trail showing the water holes, everything. Of course, it's nothing to me what route you take, but if you want to avoid Indians . . ." He shrugged.

"What about Buffalo Hide?"

Morton Harper's face tightened, and his eyes strained to pry Rock Bannon's face from the shadows in which he sat. "He's a Blackfoot. He ranges farther north." Harper's eyes shifted to Mulholland. "Who is this man? I'm surprised he should ask about Buffalo Hide, as he isn't known to most white men other than renegades. I can't understand why he should try to persuade you to neglect an easier route for a more dangerous one. Is he one of your regular train?"

Pike Purcell was abrupt. From the first day he had disliked and been suspicious of Bannon. "No, he ain't none of our crowd, just a feller what tied up with us back yonder a ways. He ain't got no wagon, nothin' but the horse he's ridin'."

"I see." Morton Harper's face became grave with implied doubt. "No offense, friend, but would you mind telling me your name? I know most of the men along this trail, and Colonel Warren was asking about some of them only tonight. You'll admit it is safer to be careful, for there are so many renegades who work with the Indians."

"My name's Rock Bannon."

Morton Harper's lips tightened and his eyes grew wary. For a moment he seemed taken aback. Then, as he perceived where his own interests lay, his eyes lighted with triumph.

"Ah? Bannon, eh? I've heard of you. Killed a man in Laramie a month or so back, didn't you?"

"He drew on me."

Rock was acutely conscious of the sudden chill in the atmosphere, and he could see Sharon's shocked gaze directed at him. The people of the wagon train were fresh from the East. Only Cap had been as far West as the Platte before, and he only once. They were peace-loving men, quiet and asking no trouble.

Morton Harper was quick to sense his advantage. "Sorry to have brought it up, Bannon," he said smoothly, "but, when a man advises a wagon train against their best interests, it is well to inquire into the source of the advice."

Bannon got up. He was a tall man, lean-hipped and broad-shouldered, his flat-brimmed hat shadowing his face, his eyes glowing with piercing light as he spoke.

"I still say that route's a darned fool way to go. This ain't no country to go wanderin' around in, and that route lays through Hardy Bishop's country. You spoke of Hastings. He was the man who advised the Donner party."

As his footsteps died away in the darkness, the members of the wagon train sat very still, their enthusiasm suddenly dampened by that ill-fated name. They all knew the story. The horror of it still blanketed the trail with its bloody shadow of the party caught by snows in the high passes and starving until they resorted to cannibalism as a way out.

Morton Harper shrugged. "Of course. They started on Hastings's trail, but left it too soon, and the route I suggest avoids all the higher passes." His eyes swung around the group, gathering their attention like the reins of a six-horse team, and he led them on with promises and suggestions, an easy flow of calm, quiet talk, stilling their fears, quieting their doubts, offering them grass and water instead of dust and desert.

In the morning, when they moved out, they took the trail Harper had advised, turning off an hour after they left the fort. Harper glanced back, and smiled when he saw he was unobserved. Then he wished them luck and promised to overtake them when a message came for which he waited. Turning, he galloped back to the fort.

Rock Bannon was with them. He rode close to Sharon's wagon, and after a time she looked up. He had watched her the night before, had seen her fascinated eyes on Harper's face.

"You don't approve, do you?"

He shook his head. Then he smiled, somewhat grimly. He was a dark, good-looking man with a tinge of recklessness in his green eyes.

"My views aren't important," he said. "I don't belong."

"Pike shouldn't have said that," she said. "He's a strange man. A good man, but very stubborn and suspicious."

"Not suspicious of the right folks, maybe."

Her eyes flashed. "You mean Mister Harper? Why should we be suspicious of him? He was only trying to help."

"I wonder."

"I think," Sharon said sharply, "you'd do better to be a little less suspicious yourself. You admitted this was a good trail."

"You haven't met Hardy Bishop yet. Nor Buffalo Hide."

"Mister Harper said that Indian was farther north." She looked at him. "Who is Hardy Bishop? You mentioned him before?"

"He's a man who is trying to run cattle at Indian Writing. They said he's insane to try it, but he's claimed seventy miles of range, and he has cattle there. We have to cross his range."

"What's wrong with that?"

"If you cross it, maybe nothing, but Bishop's a funny man. He doesn't like strangers very much. He's going to wonder why you're so far south. He's going to be suspicious."

"Well, let him be suspicious then!" Sharon said, her eyes bright and her chin lifting. "We don't care, and we won't bother him any. Does he think he owns the whole country?"

"Uhn-huh," Rock said. "I'm afraid he does. With some reason as far as that valley goes. He made it what it is today."

"How could any man make a valley?" Sharon protested. "This is all free country. Anyway, we're just going through."

The conversation had dwindled and died, and after a while he rode off to the far flank of the wagon train. Sharon's manner was distinctly stiff and he could see she was remembering that story of the killing in Laramie. After a few rebuffs he avoided her. Nobody talked to him. He rode alone and camped alone.

Chapter Two

It had remained like that for six days. They were six days during which Morton Harper's name became one to reckon with. The long green valley down which they moved was unrutted by wagon trains, the grass was green and waving, and water was plentiful. Harper's map showed an accurate knowledge of the country and was a great help. On the sixth day after leaving the fort, the Indians hit them.

The attack came at daybreak. Rock Bannon, camping near a spring a half mile from the wagons, awoke with a start. It was scarcely light, yet he felt uneasy, and, getting to his knees, he saw the steel-dust staring, ears pricked, at a distant pile of rocks. Then he noticed the movement.

Swiftly and silently he saddled the stallion, bridled it, and stowed his gear in the saddlebags. Then, rifle in hand, he skirted the trees along the tiny stream and headed back for the wagons. He rode up to them, and the man on guard got up, stretching. It was the short, heavy-set Pagones. A good man and a sharp one. He smiled at Bannon.

"Guess Harper had it more right than you when he said there were no hostiles here," he said. "Ain't that right?"

"No," Bannon said sharply. "Get everybody up and ready. We'll be attacked within a few minutes!"

Pagones stared. "Are you crazy?"

"Get busy, man!" Bannon snapped at Pagones. He wheeled and, running from wagon to wagon, slapped the canvas and said: "On your feet! Indians!"

Men boiled from the wagons, crawling into their clothes and grabbing at rifles. "Get around the whole circle!" Bannon told them. "They are in those rocks and a draw that runs along south of us."

Mulholland rushed out and halted, glaring around. The sky was gray in the east, and everything lay in a vague, indistinct light. Not a movement showed in all the dark width of the prairie. He started for Bannon to protest, when he heard a startled exclamation. Wheeling, he saw a long line of Indian horsemen not over 200 yards away and coming at a dead run!

Even as his eyes touched them, the nearest Indian broke into a wild, shrill whoop. Then the whole charging line broke into yells.

Rock Bannon, leaning against the Crockett wagon, lifted his Henry rifle and fired. A horse stumbled and went down. He fired again, and an Indian threw up his arms and vanished in the turmoil of oncoming horses and men, and then the other men of the wagon train opened up.

Firing steadily, Bannon emptied his rifle before the Indians reached the edge of the circle. One brave, his wild-eyed horse at a dead run, leaned low and shot a blazing arrow into the canvas of the Crockett wagon. Rock fired his right-hand pistol and the Indian hit the dirt in a tumbling heap, just as a second arrow knocked off Rock's hat. Reaching up with his left hand, Rock jerked the burning arrow from the canvas. The fire had not yet caught. Then he opened up, firing his pistol, shifting guns, and firing again. The attack broke as suddenly as it had begun.

Tom Crockett was kneeling behind a water barrel, his face gray. A good shot, he was not accustomed to killing. He glanced up at Rock, a sickened expression on his face.

"I never killed nothing human before," he said weakly.

"You'll get used to it out here," Rock said coldly. His eyes lifted to Sharon.

"You saved our wagon," she said.

"It might have been anybody's wagon," he said brutally, and turned away. He counted seven dead Indians on the prairie. There were probably one or two more hidden in the tall grass. He could see several dead ponies. The Indian who had shot the flaming arrow lay not more than a dozen feet away. The bullet had gone through his stomach and broken his spine.

Rock walked around. He had eyes only for the men. Cap looked frightened, but determined. Pagones had fired steadily and with skill. Bannon nodded at the short man.

"You'll do," he said grimly.

Pagones started to speak, started after him, and scowled a little. He was ashamed of himself when he realized he was pleased at the compliment.

They were good men, Rock decided. Purcell was reloading his rifle, and he looked up as Bannon passed, but said nothing. Rock walked back to the Crockett wagon. Cap was standing there, his rifle in the hollow of his arm.

"Will they come again?" he asked.

Bannon nodded. "Probably several times. This is Buffalo Hide. Those were his warriors."

"But Morton said . . . ," Crockett started to protest.

Bannon looked around, and then he pointed at the dead Indian. "You goin' to believe Morton Harper or that?" he demanded. "That Indian's a Blackfoot. I know by the moccasins."

This time they came in a circle, going around and around the wagon train. A volley of flaming arrows set two wagon tops afire. Rock stood at the end of the Crockett wagon and fired steadily, carefully, making every shot count.

Dawn came with a red, weird light flaming in the east and turned the wagon colors to flame. Guns crashed, and the air was filled with wild Indian yells and the acrid smell of gunpowder and burned canvas. Three times more they attacked, and Bannon was everywhere. Firing, firing, firing. Crockett went down with a bullet through his thigh. Bjornsen was shot through the head, and a warrior leaped from a horse into Greaves's wagon and the two men fought there until the Indian thrust a knife into Greaves's side. Bannon shot the brave with a snapped pistol shot, almost from the hip.

The last attack broke, and the sun lifted into the sky. As if by magic the Indians were gone. Rock Bannon wiped the sweat from his forehead and stared out over the plain. Buffalo Hide had lost men in this fight. At least twenty of his braves were dead, and there would be wailing and the death chant in the Blackfoot villages tonight.

Two horses and an ox had been killed. They gathered around, buried the two dead men, and butchered the ox. Rock sat on a wagon tongue alone. Cap walked over to him. The man's face was round and uncomfortable.

"Reckon you saved us, Rock," he said. "Don't rightly know how to thank you."

Bannon got up. He had been cleaning his rifle and reloading it while the men were being buried. "Don't try," he said.

Bob Sprague walked over and held out his hand. "Guess we haven't been very friendly," he said, "but you were right about the Indians."

Suddenly, boyishly Bannon grinned. "Forget it, Bob. You did a right good job with that rifle of yours."

They were the only two who mentioned it. Rock helped lift Crockett into the back of the wagon, and then harnessed the oxen. He was gone, riding out on the flank on the steel-dust when Sharon came to thank him. She looked after him, and her heart felt suddenly lost and alone.

It was late that day when they reached the dry country. The settlers did not realize the change until the dust began to rise, for in the distance it had looked much the same, only the grass was darker and there was less of it. Within a mile they were suffused in a cloud of powdery, sifting dust, stifling and irritating in the heat.

This was no desert. Merely long miles of plain where the hills receded and there was no subirrigation to keep the grass green and rich. All the following day the dust cloud hung over the wagon train, and from Mulholland's place in the van the last wagons could not even be distinguished.

Mulholland looked up at Bannon, who was riding beside him. "Harper said there was one bad stretch," he said almost apologetically.

Bannon did not reply. He alone of all the party knew what lay ahead. He alone knew how brutal the passage would be. Let them find out.

Days later, when Cap asked him to go for game, they all knew. They were still in that desert of dust and dirty brown brush. They had camped in it five days now. Their water barrels were empty, the wagons so hard to pull in the thick dust that they made only a few miles each day. It was the worst kind of tough going.

When he had killed two antelope in the hills, Rock rode back to join the party. Pagones, hunting on the other side, had killed one. Rock turned toward Sharon's wagon and swung down from the saddle. She looked up at him from over a fire of greasewood.

"Hello," she said. "We haven't seen much of you."

He took off his black, flat-brimmed hat. His

dark, curly hair was plastered to his brow with sweat.

"There are some here who don't want me talking to you," he said dryly. "Figure I'm a bad influence, I guess."

"I haven't said that!" she protested. She brushed a strand of hair from her eyes. "I like to have you riding close. It . . . it makes me feel safer."

He looked at her an instant, and then looked away. "How's your dad?"

"Better, I think. But this heat! It's so awful! How long before we get out of this dust?"

"Tomorrow night, at this rate. This bad stretch is over."

"Then we're free of that. Morton said there was only one."

He noticed that she had called Harper "Morton."

"He was wrong. You'll strike another near Salt Lake that's much worse than this. You'll never get across unless you swing back and take the old trail for Pilot Peak."

"But he said . . . ," Sharon protested.

Rock Bannon looked up at her from where he squatted on his haunches. "I know he did. I heard everything he said, and I'm still wondering what he has to gain by it. Nobody takes this route. Crossing the Salt Lake Desert by this route is suicide . . . with wagons, at least. You've all placed a lot of faith in a stranger."

"He was right, Rock. Those first six days were heaven, and from now on it should be good."

"From now on it will be good until you hit the desert," he admitted, "unless you stop."

"Unless we stop?" Sharon dished up a plate and handed it to him, and then poured the coffee. "Why?"

"Tomorrow we get into Hardy Bishop's country." Rock Bannon's face was somber.

"You always refer to him as if he were an outlaw or something awful."

"No," he said. "Bishop isn't any of those things. If you are his friend or a guest, he's one of the finest men alive. If you are an enemy or try to take something that's his, he is absolutely ruthless."

When she returned from feeding her father, she sat down beside him on the wagon tongue. The sun was down, and the dust had settled. Near a fire on the far side of the circle, Dud Kitchen was singing softly over his mandolin.

The air was cool now, and the soft music mingled in the air with the scent of wood smoke, the low champing of the horses, and the mumbling of the oxen. In the distance they could see the hills, purple with the last shadows before darkness, and shadowed with a promise of coolness after the long days of heat and dust and bitterness.

He stared away at the hills, remembering so much, worried, uncertain, wondering again about Morton Harper. What did the man have in mind? Who was he? Purcell said Harper had lent him money. Perhaps he had lent others in the wagon train money. It was not like a man to loan money and not follow it up to get back what was his. Behind all of this was a reason, and in the back of his mind Rock was afraid he knew that reason.

Sharon spoke suddenly. "What are you thinking

of, Rock? You are always so silent. You seem so bitter sometimes, and I can never understand what you have in your mind."

"It isn't anything." He had no desire to mention Harper again. "I was just thinking about this country."

"You like it, don't you?"

"Like it?" He looked up suddenly, and his eyes changed. He smiled suddenly and with warmth. "Like it? I love it. This is a man's country. And that ahead? Wait until you see Bishop's Valley. Miles upon miles of tumbling streams, waving green grass dotted with cattle.

"You should see Bishop's Valley. You go down through a deep gorge along a roaring mountain stream, and you can look up at cliffs that rise for three thousand feet, and then suddenly the gorge widens and you look down a long valley that is six or seven miles wide and all of fifty miles long.

"On each side, high mountain ridges shut it in, and here and there deep gorges and ravines cut back into those ridges and there are green meadows and tumbling waterfalls. And all the hills around are timbered to their crests. It's a beautiful country."

Sharon stared at him, enchanted. Rock had never talked like this before, and, as she listened to him tell of the hills and the wild game, of deer, elk, bear, and mountain goats, of the catbirds calling in the willows and the hillsides white with groves of silver-columned birch, she suddenly forgot where she was and who was talking.

"You seem to love it so much," she said. "Why did you ever leave?"

"It belongs to one man, to Hardy Bishop," Rock said. "He's carving a little empire there. He went there long before any other white man dreamed of anything but going on to California, before they thought of anything but getting rich from gold mines. They came through the country like a pack of vultures or wolves, taking everything, building nothing. They want only to get rich and get out.

"He was different. Once, when only a boy, he went into that valley on a trapping venture, and he was never content until he came back. He drove a herd of cattle west when there were no cattle in this country, and he got them into that valley and turned them loose. He fought Indians and outlaws, he built a dam, built a home, built irrigation ditches where he wanted them, and planted trees.

"He made the valley, and you can't blame him if he wants to keep it his way now."

Long after Sharon lay in her blankets, she thought of that and of Rock Bannon. How tall he was! And how strange! He had risen suddenly and with scarcely a word had walked into the night, and then she heard him mount his horse and ride away. Yet even as she heard the dwindling hoof beats, she heard something else, the sound of other horses drawing near. Still wondering who the riders could be, she fell asleep.

Scarcely were they moving in the morning before a black mare wheeled alongside the Crockett wagon. Flushing suddenly, Sharon saw Morton Harper, hat in hand, bowing to her.

"Good morning!" he said. "I hoped to catch up

with you before this, but by tomorrow you'll be in green country again."

"Yes, I know."

He looked at her quickly. "You know? Who told you?"

"Rock Bannon."

His face sharpened, and she could sense the irritation in the man. "Oh? Then he's still with you? I was hoping he had left you alone. I'm afraid he's not a good man."

"Why do you say that? He's been very helpful."

Harper shrugged. "I'd rather not say. You know of that killing in Laramie, and, if that were the only one, it would not matter. There are others. He has killed five or six men. He's a troublemaker wherever he goes. I'm glad Purcell and your men understand that, for it will save a lot of trouble."

He smiled at her. "You look so lovely this morning that it is unbelievable that you have come so far across the prairies. It is a pity you have so far to go. I've been thinking some of settling in this country here." He waved ahead. "It is such a beautiful land, and there is nothing in California so desirable."

Rock Bannon had heard the horses the night before, and he had reined in long enough to see them come up to the fire. Harper he recognized at once. There were two men with him, one a lean, sharp-faced man with a long nose. The other man was short, chuckleheaded, and blunt-featured. Bannon's lips tightened when he recognized Pete Zapata. The half-breed killer was notorious, a gunfighter and desperado of the worst stripe, but none of the wagon train would know that.

All that day he stayed away from the train, riding on ahead. He drank at the spring, killed an antelope and a couple of teal, and then rode back under a clump of poplars and waited for the wagon train to come up. They were already on Hardy Bishop's V Bar. Only a short distance behind the poplars, the long cañon known as Poplar Cañon ran down into Bishop's Valley.

He got up when he saw the first of the long caravan of wagons. Better than the others, he knew what this would mean and knew on how bad a trail they had started. He was standing there, close to the steel-dust stallion, when the wagons moved in.

The fresh water and green grass made everyone happy. Brown-legged children rushed downstream from where the drinking water was obtained, and there was laughter and merrymaking in the camp. Fires sprang up, and in a short time the camp was made and meals were being cooked.

Watchfully Rock saw Morton Harper seated on a saddle at Cap Mulholland's fire. With them were the sharp-featured stranger, Satterfield, Lamport, and Pagones. They were deep in a conference. In a few minutes Tom Crockett walked over to join them.

Dud Kitchen was tuning his mandolin when he saw Bannon sitting under the willows.

"All alone?" Kitchen said with a grin, and dropped on the grass beside Bannon. "Saw how you handled those guns in that Indian fight. Never saw the like. Make more tune with 'em than me with a mandolin!"

Rock chuckled. "But not so nice to hear." He nodded at the group of men around the fire. "Wonder what's up?"

Dud shrugged. "Harper's got some plan he's talkin' about. Sayin' they are foolish to go on when there's good country right here."

Rock Bannon sprang to his feet, his eyes afire with apprehension. "So that's it," he said. "I might have known it."

Kitchen was startled. "What's the matter? I think it would be a good idea myself. This is beautiful country. I don't know that I've ever seen better. Harper says that down this draw behind us there's a long, beautiful valley, all open for settlement."

But Rock Bannon was no longer listening. Stepping across the branch of the creek, he started for the fire. Morton Harper was talking when Rock walked up.

"Why not?" Harper was saying. "You all want homes. Can you find a more beautiful country than this? That dry plain is behind you. Ahead lies the Salt Lake Desert, but, in here, this is a little bit of paradise. Beyond this range of hills . . . you can reach it through Poplar Cañon . . . is the most beautiful valley you ever saw. It's just crying for people to come in and settle down. There's game in the hills and the best grazing land in the world, all for the taking."

"What about Hardy Bishop?" Bannon demanded harshly.

Harper looked up, angered. "You, again? Every time these people try to do anything, you interfere! Is it your business where they stop? Is it your business if they remain here or go on to California? Are you trying to dictate to these people?"

Pike Purcell was on his feet, and Rock could see all the old dislike in the big Missourian's face. The other men looked at him with disapproval, too. Yet he went on recklessly, heedlessly.

"Hardy Bishop settled that valley. He's running two thousand head of cattle in there. You try to settle in that valley and you're asking for trouble. He won't stand for it."

"An' we won't stand for you buttin' in!" Purcell said suddenly. He dropped a hand to the big Dragoon pistol in his holster. "I've had enough of your buttin' around, interferin' in our affairs. I'm tellin' you now, you shut up an' get out."

"Wait just a minute!" Bob Sprague stepped closer. "This man warned us about that Indian attack, or we'd all be dead, includin' you, Pike Purcell. He did more fightin' in that attack than any one of us, or two of us, for that matter. His advice has been good, and I think we should listen to him!"

Dud Kitchen nodded. "Speak up, Rock. I'll listen."

"There's little to be said," Bannon told them quietly. "Only the land this man is suggesting you settle on was settled on over ten years ago by a man who fought Indians to get it. He fought Indians and outlaws to keep it. He won't see it taken from him now in his old age. He'll fight to keep it. I know Hardy Bishop. I know him well enough to be sure that, if you move into that valley, many of the women in this wagon train will be widows before the year is out.

"What I don't know is Morton Harper's reason for urging you into this. I don't know why he urged you to take this trail, but I think he has a reason, and I think that reason lies in Bishop's Valley. You are coming West to win homes. You have no right to do it by taking what another man fought to win and to keep. There is plenty for all farther West."

"That makes sense to me," Sprague said quietly. "I for one am moving West."

"Well, I'm not," Purcell said stubbornly. "I like this country, and me and the wife have seen enough dust and sun and Indians. We aim to stay."

"That valley is fifty miles long, gentlemen," Harper said.

"I think there is room enough for us all in Bishop's Valley."

"That seems right to me," Cap said. He looked around at Tom Crockett, limping near the fire. "How about you, Tom?"

"I'm staying," Crockett said. "I like it here."

Satterfield nodded. "Reckon I'll find me a place to set up a blacksmith shop," he said. "But there's a sight of things we all need. There ain't no stores, no place to get some things we figured to get in California."

"That will be where I come in." The man with the sharp features smiled pleasantly. "I'm John Kies, and I have six wagonloads of goods coming over the trail to open a store in our new town!"

Chapter Three

Silently Rock Bannon turned away. There was no further use in talking. He caught Sharon's eye, but she looked away, her gaze drawn to Mort Harper where he sat now, talking easily, smoothly, planning the new home, the new town.

Bannon walked back to his blankets and turned in, listening to the whispering of the poplar leaves and the soft murmur of the water in the branch. It was a long time before he fell asleep, long after the last talking had died away in the wagon train and when the fires had burned low.

When daylight came, he bathed and saddled the stallion. Then, carefully, he checked his guns. At a sound, he glanced up to see Sharon Crockett dipping water from the stream.

"Good morning," he said. "Did you finally decide to stay?"

"Yes." She stepped toward him. "Rock, why are you always against everything we do? Why don't you stay, too? I'm sure Morton would be glad to have you. He's planned all this so well, and he says we'll need good men. Why don't you join us?"

"No, not this time. I stayed with the wagon train because I knew what you were going into. I wanted to help you . . . and I mean *you*. In what is to come, no one can help you. Besides, my heart wouldn't be in it."

"You're afraid of this crabby old man?" she asked scornfully. "Morton says as soon as Bishop sees we intend to stay, he won't oppose us at all. He's just crabby and difficult because he's old, and he has more land than he needs. Are you afraid of him?"

Rock smiled. "You sure set a lot of store by this Harper fellow, don't you? Did he tell you that Bishop's riders were all crabby old men, too? Did Harper tell you why he carries Pete Zapata along with him?"

"Who is he?" Sharon looked up, her eyes curious, yet resentful.

"You've called me a killer," Bannon replied. "I have killed men. I may kill more, although I hope not, but Pete Zapata, that flat-faced man who rides with Harper, is a murderer. He's a killer of the most vicious type and the kind no decent man would have near him."

Her eyes flared. "You don't think Morton Harper is decent? How dare you say such a thing behind his back?"

"I'll face him with it," Bannon said dryly. "I expect I'll face him with it more than once. But before you get in too deep, ask yourself again what he is getting out of all this? He goes in for talk of brotherly love, but he carries a gunman at his elbow."

He turned and swung into the saddle as she picked up her bucket. He reined in the horse at a call. It was Bob Sprague.

"Hey, Rock! Want to come on West with us?"

He halted. "You're going on?"

"Uhn-huh. Six wagons are going. We decided we liked the sound of what you said. We're pullin' on for California, and we'd sure admire to have you with us!"

Bannon hesitated. Sharon was walking away, her head held proudly. Did she seem to hesitate for his reply? He shrugged.

"No," he said. "I've got other plans."

Sharon Crockett, making frying-pan bread over the fire beside her wagon, stood up to watch Bob Sprague lead off six wagons, the owners of which had decided not to stay. All farewells had been said the night before, yet now that the time for leave-taking had come, she watched uneasily.

For years she had known Bob Sprague, ever since she was a tiny girl. He had been her father's friend, a steady, reliable man, and now he was going. With him went five other families, among them some of the steadiest, soberest men in the lot.

Were they wrong to take Morton Harper's advice? Her father, limping with the aid of a cane cut from the willows, walked back, and stood beside her, his face somber. He was a tall man, almost as tall as Harper and Bannon, his hair silvery around the temples, his face gray with a slight stubble of beard. He was a fearless, independent man, given to going his own way and thinking his own thoughts.

Pagones walked over to them. "Did Bannon go along? I ain't seen him."

"I don't think he went," Crockett replied. "Sprague wanted him to go."

"No, he didn't go," said Satterfield, who had walked up to join them. Satterfield had been a frontier lawyer back in Illinois. "I saw him riding off down the cañon, maybe an hour ago."

"You think there will be trouble?" Pagones asked.

Satterfield shrugged. "Probably not. I know how some of these old frontiersmen are. They hate to see civilization catch up with them, but, given time, they come around. Where's Harper?"

"He went off somewhere with that dark-lookin' feller who trails with him," Pagones said. "Say, I'm glad Dud Kitchen didn't go. I'd sure miss that music he makes. He was goin', then at the last minute changed his mind. He's goin' down with Harper and Cap to survey that town site."

"It'll seem good to have a town again," Crockett said. "Where's it to be?"

"Down where Poplar Cañon runs into Bishop's Valley. Wide, beautiful spot, they say, with plenty of water and grass. John Kies is puttin' in a store, I'm goin' to open an office, and Collins is already figurin' on a blacksmith shop."

"Father, did you ever hear of a man named Zapata?" Sharon asked thoughtfully. "Pete Zapata?"

Crockett looked at her curiously. "Why, no. Not that I recall. Why?"

"I was just wondering, that's all."

The next morning they hitched up the oxen and moved their ten wagons down Poplar Cañon to the town site. The high, rocky walls of the cañon widened slowly, and the oxen walked on, knee deep in rich green grass. Along the stream were willow and poplar, and higher along the cañon sides she saw alder, birch, and mountain mahogany, with here and there a fine stand of lodgepole pine.

Tom Crockett was driving, so she ranged alongside, riding her sorrel mare.

As they rounded the last bend in the cañon, it spread widely before them, and she saw Morton Harper sitting his black mare some distance off. Putting the sorrel to a gallop, she rode down swiftly, hair blowing in the wind. Dud Kitchen was there with Zapata and Cap. They were driving stakes and lining up a street.

Before them the valley dropped into the great open space of Bishop's Valley, and she rode on. Suddenly, rounding a knoll, she stopped and caught her breath.

The long, magnificent sweep of the valley lay before her, green and splendid in the early morning sun. Here and there over the grassland, cattle grazed, belly deep in the tall grass. It was overpowering; it was breathtaking. It was something beyond the grasp of the imagination. High on either side lifted the soaring walls of the cañon, mounting into high ridges, snowcapped peaks, and majestic walls of gray rock.

This was the cattle empire of Hardy Bishop. This was the place Rock Bannon had spoken of with such amazing eloquence.

She turned in her saddle at the sound of a horse's hoofs. Mort Harper rode up beside her, his face glowing.

"Look!" he cried. "Magnificent, isn't it? The most splendid view in the world. Surely that's an empire worth taking."

Sharon's head turned quickly, sharply. At something in Harper's eyes she caught her breath, and, when she looked again at the valley, she was uneasy.

"What . . . what did you say?" she asked. "An empire worth taking?"

He glanced at her quickly, and then laughed. "Don't pay any mind. I was thinking of Bishop, the man who claims all this. He took it. Took it from the Indians by main force." Then he added: "He's an old brute. He'd stop at nothing."

"Do you think he will make trouble for us?" she inquired anxiously.

He shrugged. "Probably not. He might, but, if he does, we can handle that part of it. Let's go back, shall we?"

She was silent during the return ride, and she kept turning over in her mind her memory of Bannon's question: *What's he going to get out of this?* Somehow, half hypnotized by Harper's eloquence, she had not really thought of that. That she thought of it now gave her a twinge of doubt. It seemed, somehow, disloyal.

* * *

For three days, life in the new town went on briskly. They named the town Poplar. Kies's store was the first building up, and the shelves were heavy with needed goods. Kies was smiling and affable. "Don't worry about payment," he assured them. "We're all in this together. Just get what you need, and I'll put it on the books. Then, when you get money from furs or crops, you can pay me."

It was easy. It was almost too easy. Tom Crockett built a house in a bend of the creek among the trees, and he bought dress goods for Sharon, trousers for himself, and bacon and flour. Then he bought some new tools.

Those first three days were hard, unrelenting labor, yet joyful labor, too. They were building homes, and there is always something warming and pleasant in that. At the end of those first three days, Kies's store was up, and so were Collins's blacksmith shop, Satterfield's office, and Harper's Saloon and Theater. All of them pitched in and worked.

Then one day, as she was leaving Kies's store, she looked up to see three strange horsemen coming down the street. They were walking their horses, and they were looking around in ill-concealed amazement.

Mulholland had come out behind her, and at the sight of him one of the horsemen, a big, stern-looking man with a drooping red mustache, reined his horse around.

"You!" he said. "What do you all think you're doin' here?"

"Buildin' us a town," Cap said aggressively. "Any objections?"

Red laughed sardonically. "Well, sir," he said, "I reckon I haven't, but I'm afraid the boss is sure goin' to raise hob."

"Who's the boss?" Cap asked. "And what difference does it make? This is all free land, isn't it?"

"The boss is Hardy Bishop," Red drawled, glancing around. He looked approvingly at Sharon, and there seemed a glint of humor in his eyes. "And you say this is free land. It is and it ain't. You see, out here a man takes what he can hold. Hardy, he done come in here when all you folks was livin' fat and comfortable back in the States. He settled here, and he worked hard. He trapped and hunted and washed him some color, and then he went back to the States and bought cattle. Drivin' them cattle out here ten years ago was sure a chore, folks, but he done it. Now they've bred into some of the biggest herds in the country. I don't think Hardy's goin' to like you folks movin' in here like this."

"Is he so selfish?" Sharon demanded. "Why, there's land here enough for thousands of people!"

Red looked at her. "That's how you see it, ma'am. I reckon to your way of thinkin' back East, that might be true. Here, it ain't true. A man's needs run accordin' to the country he's in and the job he has to do. Hardy Bishop is runnin' cows. He expects to supply beef for thousands of people. To do that he needs a lot of land. You see, ma'am, if thousands of people can't raise their own beef, somebody's got to have land enough to raise beef for all those thousands of people. And Hardy, he come by it honest."

"By murdering Indians, I suppose!"

Red looked at her thoughtfully. "Ma'am, somebody's been tellin' you wrong. Plumb wrong. Hardy never murdered no Indians."

"What's going on here?" Morton Harper stepped into the street. To his right was Pete Zapata, to his left Pike Purcell. Lamport lounged in the door of the store.

"Why, nothin', mister," Red said thoughtfully. His gaze had sharpened, and Sharon saw his eyes go from Harper to Zapata. "We was just talkin' about land and the ownership of it. We're ridin' for Bishop, and . . ."

"And you can ride right out of here!" Harper snapped. "Now!"

Sharon was closer to the Bishop riders, and suddenly she heard the second man say softly: "Watch it, Red. That's Zapata."

Red seemed to stiffen in his saddle, and his hand, which had started to slip off the pommel of the saddle with no aggressive intention, froze in position. Without a word, they turned their horses and rode away.

"That's the beginning," Harper stated positively. "I'm afraid they mean to drive us from our homes."

"They didn't sound much like trouble," Cap ventured hesitantly. "Talked mighty nice."

"Don't be fooled by them," Harper warned. "Bishop is an outlaw, or the next thing to it."

* * *

Tom Crockett was a man who loved the land. No sooner had he put a plow into the deep, rich soil of the cañon bottom than he felt he had indeed come home. The soil was deep and black, heavy with richness, land that had never known a plow. Working early and late, he had in the next day managed to plow several acres. Seed he bought from Kies, who seemed to have everything they needed.

There were several hours a day he gave to working on the buildings the others were throwing up, but logs were handy, and all but Zapata and Kies worked on the felling and notching of them. Kies stayed in his store, and Zapata lounged close by.

Morton Harper helped with the work, but Sharon noticed that he was never without a gun, and his rifle was always close by. At night in his saloon he played cards with Purcell and Lamport and anyone else who came around. Yet several times a day he managed to stop by, if only for a minute, to talk to her.

He stopped by one day when she was planting a vine near the door. He watched her for a few minutes, and then he stepped closer.

"Sharon," he said gently, "you shouldn't be doing this sort of thing. You're too beautiful. Why don't you let me take care of you?"

She looked at him, suddenly serious. "Is this a proposal?"

His eyes flashed, and then he smiled. "What else? I suppose I'm pretty clumsy at it."

"No," she returned thoughtfully, "you're not clumsy at it, but let's wait. Let's not talk about it until everyone has a home and is settled in a place of their own."

"All right," he agreed reluctantly. "But that won't be very long, you know."

It was not until they were eating supper that night that her thoughts suddenly offered her a question. What about Morton's home? He had not even started to build. He was sleeping in a room behind the saloon, such in name only as yet, for there was little liquor to be had.

The thought had not occurred to her before, but it puzzled and disturbed her. Tom Crockett was full of plans, talking of crops and the rich soil.

The next day Morton Harper was gone. Where he had gone Sharon did not know, but suddenly in the middle of the morning she realized he was not among them. The black mare was gone, too. Shortly after noon she saw him riding into town, and behind him came six wagons, loaded with boxes and barrels. They drew up before the store and the saloon.

He saw her watching and loped the mare over to her door.

"See?" he said, waving a hand. "The supplies! Everything we need for the coming year, but if we need more, I can send a rider back to the fort after more."

"Then you had them coming from the fort?" she asked. "You were far-sighted."

He laughed, glancing at her quickly. "Well, I thought these things would sell in the mining camps out in California, but this is much, much better."

In spite of herself, Sharon was disturbed. All day as she went about her work, the thought kept recurring that those supplies offered a clue to something, yet she could find nothing on which to fasten her suspicions. Why should their arrival disturb her so much? Was it unusual that the man should start several wagonloads of supplies to California?

Pagones stopped by the spring to get a drink. He smiled at her, pushing back his hat from a sweating brow.

"Lots of work, ma'am. Your pa's sure getting in his plowing in a hurry. He'll have his seed in before the rest of us have started."

"Pag, how do the supplies reach the gold fields in California?" Sharon said suddenly.

He looked up over his second dipper of water. "Why, by sea, of course. Much cheaper that way. Why do you ask? Something botherin' you?"

"Not exactly. Only ever since those wagons came in this morning, I've been wondering about them. Morton said he had started them for California, but thought they would sell better here. Why would he send them to California to sell when they can get supplies by sea?"

"Might mean a little ready money," Pagones suggested. He hung the dipper on a shrub. "Now that you mention it, it does seem kind of strange."

The expected trouble from Hardy Bishop did not materialize as soon as she expected. No other riders came near, although several times she noticed men, far out in the valley. All of Morton

Harper's promises seemed to be coming true. He had said Bishop would not bother them.

Yet all was not going too smoothly. The last wagons had brought a load of liquor, and several of the men hung around the saloon most of the time. Purcell was there every evening, although by day he worked on his place. Pete Zapata was always there when not off on one of his lonely rides, and the teamsters who had brought the wagons to Kies's store had remained, loitering about, doing nothing at all, but always armed. One of them had become the bartender.

During all this time, her work had kept Sharon close to the house and there had been no time for riding. Time and again she found herself going to the door and looking down toward the cluster of buildings that was fast becoming a thriving little village. And just as often she looked back up the trail they had followed when first coming into Poplar Cañon.

Not even to herself would she admit what she was looking for. She refused to admit that she longed to see the steel-dust stallion and its somber, lonely rider. She had overheard him say he would not leave, yet where was he?

The sound of a horse's hoofs in the trail outside brought her to the cabin door. It was Mary Pagones, daughter of George Pagones, who had long since proved himself one of the most stable men in the wagon train.

"Come on, Sharon . . . let's ride! I'm beginning to feel cramped with staying down here all the time."

Sharon needed no urging, and in a few minutes they were riding out of the settlement toward the upper reaches of the cañon.

"Have you seen that Pete Zapata staring at the women the way he does?" Mary asked. "He fairly gives me the creeps."

"Somebody said he was a gunman," Sharon ventured.

"I wouldn't doubt it!" Mary was an attractive girl, always gay and full of laughter. The freckles over her nose were an added attraction rather than otherwise. "Dud doesn't like him at all. Says he can't see why Harper keeps him around."

As they rode out of Poplar Cañon, an idea suddenly occurred to Sharon, and without voicing it she turned her mare toward their old encampment, but as they burst through the last line of trees, disappointment flooded over her. There was no sign of Rock Bannon.

They had gone almost a mile farther, when suddenly Mary reined in sharply.

"Why, look at that!" She pointed. "Wagon tracks coming out of that cañon! Who in the world would ever take a wagon in there?"

Sharon looked at them and then at the cañon. It was narrow-mouthed, the only entrance into a wild, rugged region of crags and ravines, heavily forested and forbidding. Riding closer, she looked down. The wagon tracks were coming from the cañon, not going into it. She studied the mountains thoughtfully. Then, wheeling her horse, with Mary following, she rode out on their own trail. All the tracks she had observed were old.

She looked at Mary, and Mary returned the glance, a puzzled frown gathering around her eyes. "What's the matter?" Mary asked. "Is something wrong?"

"I don't know," Sharon said. "There are no tracks here since we came over the trail, but there are tracks coming out of that cañon."

Mary's eyes widened. "You mean those wagons of Harper's? Then they must have come over a different trail."

That wasn't what Sharon was thinking, but she just shook her head. "Don't say anything about it," she said.

They rode on. That wall of mountains would not offer a trail through, and, if it did, where would it go? If it joined the Overland Trail to the north, it would still be almost twice as far as by the trail they had come, and through one of the most rugged sections she had ever seen. Suddenly she knew. Those wagons had been here before. They had been back there, in some remote cañon, waiting.

Waiting for what? For a town to begin? But that was absurd. No one had known the town would begin until a few hours before. No one, unless it had been Morton Harper.

Chapter Four

On, through hills of immeasurable beauty, the two girls rode. Great, rocky escarpments that towered to the skies and mighty crags, breasting their saw-toothed edges against the wind. Long, steep hill-sides clad with alder and birch or rising to great, dark-feathered crests of lodgepole pine mingled here and there with an occasional fir.

Along the lower hillsides and along the mountain draws were quaking aspen, mountain mahogany, and hawthorn. They had come to the edge of a grove of poplar when they saw the horseman. They both saw him at once, and something in his surreptitious manner brought them to a halt. They both recognized him at the same instant.

"Sharon," Mary said, "it's that Zapata!"

"*Ssh!* He'll hear us." Sharon held her breath. Suddenly she was frightened at the idea of being found out here, even with Mary along, by Zapata. But Zapata seemed to have no eyes for them or even their direction. He was riding by very slowly, not over fifty yards away, carrying his rifle in his hands and watching something in the valley below that was beyond their vision.

Yet, even as they watched, he slid suddenly from the saddle and crouched upon some rocks on the rim. Then he lifted his rifle and fired!

"What's he shooting at?" Mary asked in a whisper.

"I don't know. A deer, probably. Let's get home." Turning their horses, they rode back through the trees and hit the trail back to the settlement.

All the next day Sharon thought about that wagon trail out of the mountains. Several times she started to speak to her father, but he was preoccupied, lost in plans for his new home, and thinking of nothing but it. Later in the day she saw Dud Kitchen riding over. He reined in and slid from the saddle.

"Howdy, Sharon! Sure glad to see you all! We been talkin' some, Mary and I, about us gettin' up a sort of party. Seems like Satterfield plays a fiddle, and we thought we might have a dance, sort of. Liven things up a mite."

"That's a good idea, Dud," Sharon agreed. She looked up at him suddenly. "Dud, did Mary tell you anything about that wagon trail we saw?"

His blue eyes sharpened and he ran his fingers back through his corn-colored hair. "Yeah," he said, "she did."

"Dud, it looks to me like those wagons were out here before we were, just waiting. It begins to look like somebody planned to have us stop here."

"You mean Mort? But what would he do that

for? What could he gain? And even if he did, you've got to admit it's a good place."

"Yes, it is, but just the same I don't like it."

Her father was walking toward them with George Pagones and Cap Mulholland.

"What's this you young folks figurin' to do?" Cap said, grinning. "Hear we're havin' us a party."

Her answer was drowned by a sudden rattle of horses' hoofs, and she saw three men swing down the cañon trail. When they saw the group before the house, they reined in. One of them was Red, the man who had called on them the first day. Another was—her breath caught—Rock Bannon!

"Howdy!" Red said. He looked down at the men, and then recognized Cap. "Seen anything of a young feller, 'bout twenty or so, ridin' a bay pony?"

"Why, no," Cap said. "Can't say as I have. What's the trouble?"

"He's Wes Freeman, who rides for us. He was huntin' strays over this way yesterday and he never came back. We figured maybe he was hurt somehow."

"No, we haven't seen him," Crockett said.

Dud Kitchen was grinning at Rock. "Shucks, man! We figured you had left the country. What you doin'?"

Bannon grinned. "I'm ridin' for Hardy Bishop," he said. "Went over there right after I left you folks."

"What made you think your man might have come over here?" Pagones asked. "Was he ridin' thisaway?"

"As a matter of fact," Red said, "he was ridin'

back northeast of here. Pretty rough country, except for one cañon that's got some good grass in it."

The third man was short, thick-set, and tough. "Hurry up, Red," he said. "Why beat around the brush. Tell 'em."

"All right," Red said. "I'll just do that, Bat." He looked down at the little group before the house. "Fact of the matter is, Wes's horse come in about sundown yesterday, come in with blood on the saddle. We back-trailed the horse and we found Wes. We found him in the open valley we spoke of. He was dead. He'd been shot through the back and knocked off his horse. Then whoever shot him had followed him up and killed him with a hunting knife."

Zapata! Sharon's eyes widened, and she looked around to see Dud staring at her, gray-faced. She had seen Zapata shoot!

In stunned silence the men stared up at the three riders. Rock broke the silence.

"You can see what this means?" he said sternly. "Wes was a mighty nice boy. I hadn't known him as long as these men, but he seemed to be a right fine feller. Now he's been murdered . . . dry-gulched. That's going to mean trouble."

"But why come to us?" Cap protested. "Sure, you don't believe we. . . ."

"We don't believe!" Bat broke in harshly. "We know! We trailed three riders down out of those hills! Three from here! Wes was my ridin' partner. He was a durned good boy. I'm goin' to see the man who done that."

"Turn around."

The voice was cold and deadly. As one person, they turned. Pete Zapata, his guns low slung on his hips, was staring at the three riders. Flanking him were two men with shotguns, both of them from the teamsters' crowd. The other two were Lamport and Purcell of the wagon train.

Behind them, and a little to one side, was Morton Harper. He was wearing two guns.

"Get out of here!" Harper snapped harshly. "Don't come around here again, aimin' to make trouble. That's all you came for, and you know it! You've been looking for an excuse to start something so you could get us out of here, take our homes away from us. Now turn your horses and get out!"

His eyes riveted on Rock Bannon. "As for you, Bannon," he said sharply, "you're a traitor! You rode with us, and now you've gone over to them. I think you're the cause of all this trouble. If a man of yours is dead, I think it would be a good idea if these friends of yours back-trailed you. Now get moving, all of you!"

"This is a bad mistake, Harper," Rock said evenly. "I'm speaking of it before all these people." He nodded at the group in front of the house. "Bishop was inclined to let 'em stay, despite the fact that he was afraid they'd bring more after them. He listened to me and didn't run you off. Now you're asking for it."

"He listened to *you!*" Harper's voice was alive with contempt. "You? A trail runner?"

Red looked quickly at Rock and started to speak. Bannon silenced him with a gesture.

"We'll ride, Harper, but we want the man . . . or men . . . who killed Wes. And we want him delivered to us by sundown tomorrow. If not, we'll come and get him."

Turning abruptly, they started away. Wheeling, Zapata grabbed a shotgun from one of the teamsters. "I'll fix him, the bluffer!"

"Hold it!" Pagones had a six-shooter and was staring across it at Zapata. "We don't shoot men in the back."

For an instant, they glared at each other. Then Harper interposed. "Put it down, Pete. Let them go." He looked around. "There'll be a meeting at the saloon tonight. All of you be there."

When they had all gone, Tom Crockett shook his head sadly. "More trouble, and all because of that Bannon. I almost wish we'd let him die on the trail."

"It wasn't Bannon, Father," Sharon said. "Those men were right, I think. Mary and I saw Zapata yesterday. Two of the horses they trailed back here were ours. The other one was his. We were not fifty yards away from him when he fired that shot. We didn't see what he shot at, but it must have been that man."

Crockett's face was gray. "Are you sure, Sharon? Are you positive?"

"Yes, I am."

"Then we must give him up," he said sadly. "If he killed, he should suffer for it. Especially if he killed that way." He got up and reached for his hat. "I must go and tell Morton. He'll want to know."

She put a hand on his arm. "Father, you mustn't. Don't say anything to him until you've told the others. Pagones, I mean, and Cap. I'm afraid."

"Afraid of what? Morton Harper is a fine man. When he knows what happened, he'll want something done himself."

Putting on his hat, he started across the road for the cluster of buildings. Only for an instant did she hesitate. Then she swung around and ran to her horse, standing saddled and bridled as she had planned to ride over to Mary's. Dud Kitchen would be there, and Pagones.

They were sitting at the table when she burst into the room.

"Please come!" she said when she had explained. "I'm afraid!"

Without a word, they got up and buckled on their guns. It was only a few hundred yards to the saloon, and they arrived just a few moments after Tom Crockett had walked up to Harper.

"Morton, my daughter and Mary Pagones saw Zapata fire that shot yesterday," Crockett was saying. "I think we should surrender him to Bishop. We don't want to have any part in any killings."

Harper's face hardened and he started to speak. Zapata, overhearing his name, stepped to the door, his hand on a gun. Then Harper's face softened a little, and he shrugged.

"I'm afraid they were mistaken," he said carelessly. "You're being needlessly excited. Probably Pete was up that way, for he rides around a good deal, the same as the girls do. But shoot a man in the back? He wouldn't do it."

"Oh, but he did," Dud Kitchen interrupted. "What the girls say is true."

"You call me a liar?" Harper turned on him, his face suddenly flushed with anger.

"No," Kitchen replied stiffly, his face paling. "I ain't callin' no man a liar, 'specially no man who come over the trail with me, but I know what I seen with my own eyes. Mary, she done told me about that, and I'll admit I figured there was something wrong with what she said, so I went up and back-trailed 'em. I didn't have no idea about no killin' then, but I trailed the girls, and then I trailed Pete. Pete Zapata stalked that cowhand for two miles before he got the shot he wanted. I went over every inch of his trail. He was fixin' to kill him. Then I trailed him down to the body. I seen where he wiped his knife on the grass, and I seen some of them brown sort of cigarettes he smokes. Pete Zapata killed that man, sure as I'm alive."

Zapata had walked, cat-footed, to the edge of the wide plank porch in front of the saloon. He stood there now, staring at Dud.

"Trailed me, huh?" His hand swept down in a streaking movement before Dud could as much as move. His gun bellowed, and Dud Kitchen turned halfway around and dropped into the dust.

"Why, Mort!" Crockett's face was gray. "What does this mean? I . . ."

"You'd better all go back to your homes," Harper said sternly. "If Pete Zapata shot that man, and I don't admit for a minute that he did, he had a reason for it. As for this shooting here, Kitchen was wearing a gun, and he accused Zapata of murder."

Pagones's face was hard as stone. Two of the teamsters stood on the porch with shotguns. To have lifted a hand would have been to die.

"That settles it," Pagones said. "You can have your town! I'm leaving!"

"I reckon that goes for me, too," Crockett said sadly.

"I'm afraid you can't go," Harper said smoothly. There was a glint of triumph in his eyes. "My friend, John Kies, has lent you all money and supplies. Unless you can repay him what you owe, you'll have to stay until you have made a crop. California is a long ways away, and he couldn't be sure of collecting, there.

"Besides," he added, "Indians have rustled some of our stock. I have been meaning to tell you. Most of your oxen are gone." He shrugged. "But why worry? Stay here. This land is good, and these little difficulties will iron themselves out. There are always troubles when a new community begins. In a few years all this will be over and there will be children born here, a church built, and many homes."

Dud Kitchen was not dead. In the Pagones' house, Mary sat beside his bed. Satterfield had removed the bullet, and he sat at the kitchen table, drinking coffee.

"He's got him a chance," Satterfield said. "A good chance. I'm no doctor, just picked up a mite when I was in that Mexican War, but I think he'll come through."

Pagones, his heavy head thrust forward on his thick neck, stared into the fire, somber, brooding. He turned and looked at Satterfield and Crockett.

"Well," he said, "it looks bad. Looks like we're in a fight whether we want it or not. Hardy Bishop hasn't bothered us none, even after all of Mort Harper's preaching about him. Now Zapata has killed one of his men."

"That Red feller," Satterfield muttered, half to himself, "he don't look like no man to have trouble with. Nor Bat, neither."

"Where does Rock stand?" Pagones demanded. "That's what I'm wonderin'."

"Said he was ridin' for Bishop," Satterfield replied. "That's plain enough."

"If we'd listened to him, this wouldn't have happened," Mary said.

There was no reply to that. The three men stood quietly, listening to Dud Kitchen's heavy breathing. The rap at the door startled them, and they looked up to see Rock Bannon standing there.

Sharon drew in her breath, and she watched him, wide-eyed, as he stepped into the room and closed the door after him. Hat in hand, his eyes strayed from them to the wounded man lying in the bed.

How tall he was! And his shoulders had seemed to fill the door when he entered. He wore buckskin trousers tucked into hand-tooled star boots and a checked shirt with a buckskin jacket, Mexican fashion, over it. On his hips were two big Dragoon Colts in tied-down holsters.

"He hurt bad?" he asked softly.

"Yes, but Jim Satterfield says he's got a chance," Mary replied.

Rock Bannon turned to look at them. "Well," he said, "you saw me ride in here today. You know I'm riding for Bishop. From what's happened, I reckon you know that war's been declared. You've got to make up your mind whose side you are on. I talked Hardy Bishop into lettin' you stay on against his better judgment. He was all for runnin' you off *pronto*, not because he had anything against you, but because he could see settlers gettin' a toehold in his domain.

"Now one of our boys has been killed. Even Bishop might have trouble holdin' the boys back after that. I've talked to 'em, and they want the guilty man. They don't care about nobody else. What happens now is up to you."

"Not necessarily," Pagones objected. "We'll call a vote on it."

"You know how that'll go," Bannon objected. "Ten of you came in here with Mort Harper. Then he brought in Kies and Zapata. Now he's got other men. Supposin' you three vote to turn over the guilty man. How many others will vote that way? Cap may think right, but Cap will vote pretty much as Harper says. So will Purcell and Lamport. Anyway you look at it, the vote is going to be to fight rather than turn Zapata over."

"No way to be sure of that," Satterfield objected. "Harper may decide to turn him over."

Bannon turned, his temper flaring. "Haven't you learned anything on this trip? Harper's using you. He brought you down here for his own reasons.

He's out to steal Bishop's Valley from Hardy . . . that's what he wants. You're just a bunch of dupes!"

"You got any proof of that?" Crockett demanded.

"Only my eyes," Rock admitted, "but that's enough. He owns every one of you, lock, stock, and barrel. I heard about that matter of you being in debt to Kies. Don't you suppose he planned all that?"

The door opened and Mulholland came in. With him was Collins. Cap's face flushed when he saw Rock.

"You'd better light out. If Pete Zapata sees you, he'll kill you."

"That might not be so easy," Bannon said sharply. "All men don't die easy. Nor do they knuckle under to the first smooth talker who sells them a bill of goods."

Mulholland glared at him. "He promised us places, and we got 'em. Who's this Bishop to run us off? If it comes to war, then we'll fight."

"And die for Morton Harper? Do you think he'll let you keep what you have if he gets control of this valley? He'll run you out of here without a penny. You're his excuse, that's all. If the law ever comes into this, he can always say that Bishop used violence to stop free American citizens from settling on the land."

"That's just what he's doin'," Cap said. "If he wants war, he can have it!"

"Then I'd better go," Rock said. "I came here hopin' to make sóme peace talk. It looks like Zapata declared war for you. Now you've got to fight Mort Harper's war for him."

"You were one of us once," Pagones said. "You helped us on the trail. Why can't you help us now?"

Rock Bannon looked up. His eyes hesitated on Sharon's face, and then swept on. "Because you're on the wrong side," he said simply.

Sharon looked up and her eyes flashed.

"But you were one of us," she protested. "You should be with us now. Don't you understand loyalty?"

"I was never one of you after Mort Harper came," he said. Sharon flushed under his gaze. "Whatever I might have been, Harper took away from me. I ain't a smooth-talkin' man. Guess I never rightly learned to say all I feel, but sometimes them that says little feels a sight more." He put one hand on the latch. "As for loyalty, my first loyalty's to Hardy Bishop," he said.

"But how could that be?" Sharon protested.

"He's my father," Rock said quietly, and then he stepped quickly and silently out the door.

"His father!" Pagones stared after him. "Well, I'll be danged!"

"That don't cut any ice with me," Mulholland said. "Nor his talk. I got the place I want, and I aim to keep it. Harper says there ain't any way they can drive us off. He says we've got guns enough to hold our own, and this cañon ain't so easy to attack. I'm glad it's comin' to a showdown. We might as well get it over."

"All I want is to get to work," Collins said stubbornly. "I got a sight of it ahead, so if that Bishop aims to drive me off, I wish he'd come and get it over with."

"All that talk about him usin' us," Satterfield said uneasily. "That didn't make sense!"

"Of course not!" Cap said hotly. "Bannon was against everything we tried to do, right from the start. He just never had no use for Mort Harper, that was all."

"Maybe there is something to what he says," Sharon interposed.

Cap glanced around irritably. "Beggin' your pardon, Sharon. This is man's talk."

"I'm not so sure," she flashed. "We women came across the plains with you! If we fight, my father may die. That makes it important to me, and, if you think I'm going to stand by and let my home be turned into a shambles, you're wrong."

Her father started to speak, but she stepped forward. "Bannon said Harper was using you. Well, maybe he is and maybe he isn't, but there are a few things I'd like you to think about, because I've been thinking about them.

"Did Mort Harper look for this town site? No, he rode right to it, and to me that means he had planned it before. What affair was it of his which trail we took? Yet he persuaded us, and we came down here. Who got us to stay? It was him! I'll admit, I wanted to stay, and most of us did, but I'm wondering if he didn't count on that. And what about those wagons of supplies that turned up just at the right time?"

"Why, they just follered him on from the fort," Mulholland protested.

"Did they?" Sharon asked. "Go up and look at the trail. Mary and I looked at it, and no wagons have come over it since we did. Anyway, would he let those wagons come across that Indian country without more protection than they had? Those wagons were already here, waiting for us. They were back up in a cañon northeast of the trail."

"I don't believe that!" Collins said.

"Go look for yourselves then," Sharon said.

"You sound like you are against us," Cap said. "Whose side are you on, anyway?"

"I'm on the side of the wagon train people, and you know it," she said. "But a lot of this doesn't look too good to me. The first day we were here I rode down in the valley with Mort, and he said something that had me wondering, something about taking it for himself."

"Don't make sense," Cap said stubbornly. "Anyway, womenfolks don't know about things like this."

Sharon was angry. In spite of herself, and knowing her anger only made Cap more stubborn, she said: "You didn't think there were any Indians, either. You took Mort's word for that. If it hadn't been for Bannon, we'd all have been killed."

She turned quickly and went out of the cabin. Swinging into the saddle, she started across toward her own cabin. It was dark, and she could see the light in the saloon and the lights in Collins's blacksmith shop, where his wife and little Davy would be waiting for him to return.

Angry, she paid little attention where she was going until suddenly a horseman loomed in the dark near her. "Howdy!" he said, swinging alongside.

From his voice and bulk she knew him at once as Hy Miller, a big teamster who sometimes served as relief bartender. He had been drinking and his breath was thick.

She tried to push on, but he reached out and grabbed her wrist. "Don't be in no such hurry," he said, leering at her in the dimness. "I want to have a bit of palaver with you."

"Well, I don't want to talk to you!" she said angrily. She tried to jerk her wrist away, but he only tightened his grip. Then he pulled her to him and slid his other arm around her waist. She struggled, and her mare side-stepped, pulling her from the saddle.

Miller dropped her, and then slid from his own horse and grabbed her before she could escape. "I'll learn you a thing or two!" he said hoarsely. "It's about time you settlers were learnin' who's runnin' this shebang!"

What happened next, Sharon scarcely knew. She was suddenly wrenched from Miller's arms. She heard the crack of a blow, and Miller went down into the grass underfoot.

"Run for the house!" It was Bannon's voice. "Quick!"

Miller came up with an oath, and she saw him charge. Bannon smashed his left into the big teamster's mouth and staggered him, but the man leaped in, swinging with both hands. There was no chance for science or skill. In the dimness the two men fought like animals, tooth and nail, yet Bannon kept slamming his right to the bigger man's stomach. The teamster coughed and gasped, and then Rock swung a right to his chin that staggered him, and followed it up with a right and a left. Miller went down, and Bannon stooped and grasped his shirt collar in his left hand.

Holding the man at arm's length in a throttling grip, Bannon smashed him in the face again and again. Then he struck him in the body, and hurled him to the ground.

Sharon, wide-eyed and panting, still stood there. "Get to your house," Bannon snapped. "Tell your father to go armed, always. This is only the beginning."

As she fled, swiftly mounting her horse, somebody said: "Hey, what's goin' on here?"

Behind her, there was a pound of horse's hoofs, and she knew Rock was gone. Swiftly, when she reached the house, she stripped the saddle from the mare and turned her in the corral. Then she went into the house and lighted the lamp. A few minutes later, her father came in. She told him all that had happened.

He stood there, resting his fists on the table. Then he straightened.

"Honey," he said, "I'm afraid I did wrong to stop here. I wish now I'd gone on with Bob Sprague and the others. They'd be 'most to California by now. I'm afraid . . . I'm afraid!"

Chapter Five

Rock Bannon stopped that night in a line cabin six miles west of Poplar and across the valley. When morning came, he was just saddling up when Bat Chavez rode in. With him were Johnny Stark and Lew Murray. All three were armed.

Bat grinned at him. Then his eyes fell on the skinned knuckles, and he chuckled.

"Looks like you had some action."

"A little," Rock said, and then explained briefly. "You watch yourselves," he said, "and stick together. That outfit's out for trouble."

"All I want's a shot at Zapata," Bat said harshly. "I'll kill him if I get it."

Rock mounted and rode north toward the ranch house. No act of his could avert trouble now. He had hoped to convince the settlers who came with the wagon train that they should break away from Mort Harper.

That would draw the lines plainly—the ranch against the land-grabbers. That Mulholland was an honest if stupid man, he knew. The others of the train, to a man, were honest, but some of them, such as Purcell and Lamport, were firm adherents of Harper's and believed in him. This belief they combined with a dislike of Rock Bannon.

It had been a hard task to persuade Hardy Bishop to let them stay. The old man was a fire-eater, and he knew what it would mean to let settlers get a toehold in his rich valley. Once in, they would encroach more and more on his best range until he was crowded back to nothing. Only his affection for Rock had convinced him, and the fact that he had gleaned from Rock's talk that among the settlers was a girl.

Rock Bannon knew what the old man was thinking. Lonely, hard-bitten, and tough, Bishop was as affectionate as many big bear-like men are. His heart was as big and warm as himself, and from the day he had taken Rock Bannon in when the boy had been orphaned at six, when Kaw Indians had killed his parents, Bishop had lived as much for Bannon as for his ranch. Now, more than anything, he wanted Rock settled, married, and living on the broad acres of Bishop's Valley.

It had been that as much as anything that had brought him around to Rock's way of thinking when Rock had planned to go east to Council Bluffs. Secretly he had hoped the boy would come back with a wife; certainly, there were no women around Bishop's Valley but an occasional squaw. He had never seen this girl with the wagon train, but he had gleaned more than a little from Rock's casual comments, and what he heard pleased him.

Hardy Bishop was a big man, weighing nearly 300 pounds now that he was heavy around the middle. Yet in the days of his raw youth he had tipped the beam at no less than 250 pounds. On his hip even the big Dragoon Colts looked insignificant, and he was scarcely less fast than Rock.

Seated deep in a cowhide-covered chair, he looked up when Rock came in, and grinned. He was just filling his pipe. There was a skinned place on Bannon's cheekbone, and his knuckles were raw.

"Trouble, you've had," Bishop said, his deep voice filling the room. "Been over to look at them settlers again? Think they killed Wes?"

"Not the settlers," Rock said. "One of the men with them."

He sat down on the butt of a log and quietly outlined the whole situation, explaining about Harper, Zapata, and the teamsters.

"They had that stuff cached in the hills," Rock went on. "Red Lunney spotted it some time back. There were about a dozen men holed up back there with a lot of supplies, too many for themselves. He kept an eye on them, but they didn't wander around and made no trouble, so he left them alone.

"Evidently Mort Harper had them planted there. The wagon train, as near as I can figure, he planned to use as a blind in case the government got into this. He could always say they were honest settlers looking for homes, and the government would be inclined to favor them. What he really wants is Bishop's Valley."

"He'll have a time gettin' it," Bishop said grimly. "I'll bank on that. I fought Indians all over these hills, but this here valley I bought fair and square from old War Cloud. We never had no Indian trouble until lately, when the wagon trains started comin' through. Those Mormons, they had the right idea. Treat Indians good, pay for what you get, and no shootin' Indians for the fun of it, like some folks do. Why, Rock, I trapped all over these here mountains. Lived with Indians, trapped with them, hunted with them, slept in their teepees. I never had trouble with them. I was through this country with Wilson Price Hunt's Astorians when I was no more'n sixteen, but a man growed. I was with John Day in this country after that, and he saw more of it than any other man.

"Took me two years to drive these cattle in here. First ever seen in this country! I drove them up from Santa Fé in six or seven of the roughest drives any man ever saw, with Indians doin' most of my drivin' for me. They said I was crazy then, but now my cattle run these hills and they eat this valley grass until their sides are fit to bust. One of these days you'll start drivin' these cattle east. Mark my words, there'll come a day they'll make you rich. And then some whippersnapper like this Harper . . . why . . . !" He rubbed his jaw irritably, and then looked up at Rock. "You see that girl? That Crockett girl?"

"Uhn-huh," Rock admitted. "I did."

"Why not stop this here cayusin' around and bring her home, Son? Time you took a wife. Ain't no sense in a man runnin' loose too long. I did, and then hadn't my wife very long before she died. Fine girl, too."

"Hardy," Rock said suddenly, calling him by his first name as he had since Bishop first took him in hand as a child, "I don't want war with those people. They are askin' for it, and that Mulholland is simple enough to be led by the nose by Harper. Why don't you let me go get Zapata? I'll take him on myself. In fact," he added grimly, "I'd like to! Then we can take some of the boys, get Harper and his teamsters, and start them out of here."

"Separate the sheep from the goats, eh?" Bishop looked at him quizzically. "All right, Son. I've gone along with you this long. You take the boys, you get that Harper out of there, and start him back for Laramie.

"As for Zapata, do what you like. I've seen some men with guns, and you're the fastest thing I ever did see, and the best shot. But don't leave him alive. If I had my way, we'd string every one of 'em to a poplar tree, and right quick."

The old man grinned briefly at Bannon, leaned back, and lighted his pipe. So far as he was concerned, the subject was closed.

Bat Chavez was a man who made his own plans and went his own way. Loyal to the greatest degree, he obeyed Rock Bannon and Hardy Bishop without question. They were his bosses, and he liked and respected them both. However, he had another loyalty, and that was to the memory of Wes Freeman.

He and Wes had ridden together, hunted together, fought Indians together. Wes was younger, and Bat Chavez had always considered himself the other's sponsor, as well as his friend. Now Wes was dead, and to Bat Chavez that opened a feud that could only be settled by blood.

Johnny Stark and Lew Murray were like-minded. Both were young, hardy, and accustomed to live by the gun. They understood men like Zapata. Of the three, perhaps the only one who rated anything like an even break with Zapata was the half-Mexican, half-Irish Chavez. However, no one of them would have hesitated to draw on sight.

They weren't looking for trouble, but they were ready. In that frame of mind they started down the valley to move some of the cattle away from the mouth of Poplar Cañon. No one of them knew what he was riding into, and had they known, no one of them would have turned back. . . .

Mort Harper, seated in his own living quarters in the back of the saloon, was disturbed. Things had not gone as he had planned. Secure in his familiarity with men of Hardy Bishop's type, he had been positive that the arrival of the wagon train and the beginning of their settlement would precipitate trouble. He had counted on a sudden attack by Bishop and perhaps the killing of one or more of the settlers. Nothing more, he knew, would have been required to unite them against the common enemy. Peace-loving they might be, but they were men of courage and men who believed in independence and equal rights for all. Typically American, they wouldn't take any pushing around.

On his knowledge of their character and that of Bishop he had built his plans. Over a year before he had seen Bishop's Valley, and the sight had aroused a lust for possession that he had never known could live within him. Since that day he had lived for but one thing—to possess Bishop's Valley, regardless of cost.

It was beyond the reach of law. Few people in the country had any idea the valley existed or that it had been settled. His first thought was to ride in with a strong band of outlaws recruited from the off scourings of the border towns and take the place by main force, but times, he knew, were changing.

Morton Harper was shrewd enough to understand that the fight might arouse government inquiry. Frémont and Carson knew this country, and it was possible the Army might soon move into it. It would behoove him to have justice on his side.

The wagon trains offered that chance. From the first he had seen what a good chance it was. At the fort he watched them go through, and he saw the weariness of the women and children, the haggard lines of the men's faces. The novelty of the trip was over, and miles upon miles remained before they could reach Oregon. Now, if he could but get some of them into the valley country, he believed he could persuade them, by some method, to stay on. With that end in view, he watched until he saw the wagon train he wanted.

Those who were led by able and positive men he avoided. He talked to a number, but when he encountered Cap Mulholland, he was quick to perceive his opportunity.

In his visit to the camp he noted that Tom Crockett was a mild, tolerant man, friendly, and interested mainly in finding a new home and getting a plow into the ground. Pagones was a strong, able man, but not outspoken, or likely to push himself into a position of leadership.

Pike Purcell and Lamport were honest, able men, but ignorant and alike in their dislike of Rock Bannon. Lamport, who was unmarried and thoroughly undesirable, had fancied himself for an inside track with Sharon Crockett until Bannon joined the train.

As Rock Bannon was constantly with her, first as a wounded man needing care and later as a rider, Lamport grew jealous. Purcell, married to a nagging wife, had looked after Sharon with desire. His own dislike of Bannon stemmed from the same source, but grew even more bitter because Pike sensed Bannon was the better man. Pike hated him for it.

Mort Harper was quick to curry the favor of these two. He talked with them, flattered them in subtle fashion, and bought them drinks. He learned that Purcell was desperately hard up and lent him some money. He gave Lamport a gun he had admired.

The only flaw in the picture had been Rock Bannon, and, in Rock, Harper was quick to recognize a formidable and dangerous antagonist. He also realized he had an excellent weapon in the veiled enmity of Purcell and Lamport.

His plans had gone ahead very well until an attack by Bishop failed to materialize. Despite himself, he was disturbed. Would the old man really let them settle there? He caused a few cattle to be killed for meat and left evidence about. That Rock Bannon had found the remains of the slaughtered cattle and buried them, he could not know. The expected attack failed to come and he sensed a falling away from him on the part of the settlers.

The only way he could hope to get the valley was by precipitating open warfare, killing all of the Bishop forces, and taking possession. Then in due time he could eliminate the settlers themselves and reign supreme, possessor of one of the largest cattle empires in the country.

Pete Zapata was under no orders to kill, but the fact that he had killed Wes Freeman fell in line with Harper's plans. Yet he could sense the disaffection among the settlers. Crockett and Pagones could be a strong force against him if they became stubborn. Something was needed to align them firmly on his side.

That chance came, as he had hoped it would come. With Pete Zapata, Hy Miller, Pike Purcell, Lamport, and Collins, he was riding down into the valley when they saw Bat Chavez and the two Bishop riders approaching. Had Harper continued with his party along the trail on which they had started, the paths of the two groups would not have intersected, but Harper reined in and waited.

Chavez wasn't the man to ride around trouble. In Lew Murray and Johnny Stark he had two companions who had never ridden around anything that even resembled trouble. With guns loosened in holsters they rode on.

"Howdy!" Bat Chavez said. His eyes swung and fastened on Pete Zapata. "Where you ridin'?"

"Who's askin'?" Purcell demanded truculently. "We go where we want."

"Not on this range, you don't! You stick to your valley. This here's Bishop range."

"He own everything?" Miller demanded. "We ride where we please!"

"Looks like you been ridin' where somebody else pleased," Johnny Stark said, grinning. "In fact, that face looks like somebody rid all over you with spikes in his boots."

Miller's face flamed. "There was three of 'em!" he snapped. "You couldn't do it. I think it's time we taught you Bishop riders a lesson, anyways."

"You mean," Chavez demanded insolently, "like that murderin' Zapata killed Wes Freeman . . . in the back?"

Zapata's hand flashed for his gun, and Chavez was scarcely slower. Only the jerk of Zapata's horse's head saved him, as the horse took the bullet right through the head. It leaped straight up into the air, jerking Zapata's gun and spoiling his aim.

There was a sudden flurry of gunshots, and Mort Harper was quick to sense his chance. He drew his six-shooter and calmly shot Collins through the back.

The attack broke as quickly as it had begun. Zapata's horse had leaped and then hit the ground, stone dead. Thrown from the horse, Zapata lost his gun and sprawled in the grass, showing no desire to get up and join the fight or even hunt for his gun.

Outnumbered, and with Murray shot through

the leg, the Bishop riders drew off. Purcell had been burned along the cheek, and Miller's horse was killed, so the battle ended after only a few seconds with two horses and one man dead. In the excitement, only Mort Harper had seen the flare of pained astonishment and accusation in Collins's eyes.

The blacksmith's mouth refused to shape words, and he died there in the grass. Harper looked down at him, a faint smile on his face. Collins had been a popular man, quiet and well-liked. This would do what all Harper's other plans had failed to do.

"Collins got it." Pike stood over him, his hard face saddened. "He was a good man." Collins was the only man in the wagon train Pike Purcell had known before the trip began. They had come through the war together.

"Might as well bury him, I guess," Mort said.

Pike looked up. "No, we'll tote him back home. His widow will be wantin' to see him. Reckon it'll go hard with her."

Mort Harper's lips thinned, but there was nothing more he could say without arousing suspicion. Silently the little cavalcade started back. Collins's body was tied to Pike's horse, and Pike walked alongside, trailed by Zapata and Miller.

For two days ominous quiet hung over the town of Poplar. Collins had been buried, and the faces of the settlers as they gathered about to see his body lowered into the grave proved to Harper how right he had been. No longer was there any doubt or hesitation. Now they were in the fight. He had walked back from that grave filled with triumph. Only a few days longer, and then he would begin the war in earnest.

Tom Crockett was a quiet man, but his face was stern and hard as he walked back home beside Sharon.

"Well, we tried to avoid it, but now it's war," he said. "I think the sooner we have some action the better."

Sharon said nothing, but her heart was heavy within her. She no longer thought of Mort Harper. His glamour had faded, and, always now, there was but one man in her thoughts, the tall, shy, hesitant Rock Bannon.

She always marveled that a man so hard, so sure of himself when with men, horses, or guns, could be so quiet and diffident with women. As a matter of fact, Rock Bannon had never seen any woman but an Indian squaw until he was eighteen years old, in Santa Fé.

Rock Bannon had never talked to a woman until he was twenty. In his life until now, and he was twenty-seven, he had probably talked to no more than six or seven women or girls.

With deepening sadness and pain, she realized that the killing of Collins had done all they had hoped to avoid. There would be war now, and, knowing her father as she did, she knew the unrelenting stubbornness in him once he was resolved upon a course.

She had seen him like this before. He always sought to avoid trouble, always saw the best in people, yet when the battle line was laid down, no man would stay there longer than Tom Crockett.

Only one man was silent on the walk back from the grave. Dud Kitchen, weak and pale from his own narrow escape, was out for the first time. He was very tired, and he was glad when he was back in the Pagones' house and could lie down and rest. He was up too soon, he knew that, but Collins had been his friend. Now, lying alone in the gathering darkness and hearing the low mutter of men's voices in the other room, he was sorry he had gone.

He had been over to the Collins house to see his old friend once before he was buried, and he was there when the widow and Satterfield had dressed him in his Sunday go-to-meeting clothes. He saw something then that filled the whole inside of him with horror. He saw not only that Collins had been shot in the back, but something more than that, and it was that thing that disturbed him.

Dud Kitchen was a friendly, cheerful young man who liked nothing better than to sing and play the mandolin. Yet in his life from Missouri to Texas, he had had more than a little experience with guns. Once, too, he had gone down the river to New Orleans, and he had learned things on that trip.

Among other things, he knew that the Dragoon Colt had the impact of an axe and would blow a hole in a man big enough to run a buffalo through, or so it was phrased on the frontier. The hole in Collins had been small at the point of entry, but it had been wide and ugly at the point of exit.

Opening the door between the living room and the kitchen of the Pagones' house, Pike walked in to look down at Dud. "Better get yourself well, Dud," Pike said. "We'll need all hands for this fuss."

"Was it bad, Pike?" Kitchen asked. His voice was faint, and in the dim light Pike could not see what lay in the younger man's eyes.

"No, I figger it wasn't so bad," Pike said. "Only a few shots fired. It was over so quick I scarce got my gun out. That Bat Chavez, him and Zapata were fastest, but Pete's horse swung around and spoiled his aim for him. Guess it saved his life, though, 'cause Bat's bullet hit the horse right in the head. Between the eyes.

"The horse reared up and throwed Pete, and I jumped my horse away to keep from gettin' in a tangle. Lamport, he scored a shot on one of them other fellers. We seen him jerk and seen the blood on him as they were ridin' off."

Dud Kitchen waited for a long moment, and then he said carefully: "Who killed Collins?"

Purcell seemed to scowl. "Don't rightly know. There was a sight of shootin' goin' on. Might have been any one of them three. Don't you worry about that. We'll get all three of them, so we won't miss gettin' the right one."

"Have they got good guns?" Dud asked. "I'll bet they have!"

"Same as us. Dragoon Colts. One of 'em had an old Walker, though. Big gun, too. Shoots like a rifle."

After Pike Pursell was gone, Dud Kitchen lay alone in the dark room, thinking. His thoughts frightened him, and yet he was himself down from a shot by Zapata, who was on their own side. Collins had been shot in the back.

Whatever he had been shot by, Dud Kitchen was willing to take an oath it had not been by either a Walker or a Dragoon Colt. The hole was much too small, although the chest of the man had been frightfully torn. Sometimes men cut their bullets off flat across the nose to make them kill better. Dud had seen that done. It usually tore a man up pretty bad.

Chapter Six

Johnny Stark brought the news of the fight to Rock Bannon. He was with Bishop at the time, and the old man's face hardened.

"Well, there it is, Rock. We can't give them any more time now. They've had their chance, and from now on she'll be open warfare." Bishop looked up at Stark. "Take six men back with you. Have Monty go with the buckboard and bring Lew here to the ranch house where he can have proper care. You tell Red I want to see him, but he'll be in charge when he goes back."

Rock got up and paced the floor. He ran his fingers through his shock of black, curly hair. His face was stern and hard. He knew what this meant. One man had gone down, Johnny said. From his description of the man it would be Collins, one of the good men. That would serve to unite the settlers in a compact lot. Despite all his desires to avoid trouble, they were in for it now, and it would be a case of dog eat dog. What would Sharon think of all this?

Hastily he computed the numbers at the town site. Their numbers were still slightly inferior to those on the Bishop Ranch, but, because of expected Indian trouble and the stock, many of the Bishop hands must remain on the far ranges.

"I'm going out," he said at last. "I'm going down to Poplar. Also, I'm going to have a look in that cañon where Harper's stuff was cached."

"You watch yourself, boy," Bishop said. He heaved himself up in his chair. "You take care! I'm figurin' on you havin' this ranch, and I ain't wantin' to will it to no corpse."

Rock hurried down to the corral and saw Johnny Stark leading out the steel-dust, all saddled and ready.

"I figured you'd be ridin', Rock," he said grimly. He handed the reins to him and started to turn away, but then he stepped back.

"Rock," he said, "somethin' I been goin' to tell somebody. I forgot to mention it back there. Rock, I don't think any of us killed Collins!"

Bannon wheeled and grabbed the cowhand by the arm. His eyes were like steel.

"What do you mean? Give it to me quick!"

"Hey!" Johnny said. "Ease up on that arm!" He grinned. "You got a grip like a bear trap." He rubbed his arm. "Why, I been thinkin' about that ever since. Bat, he was thinkin' only of Zapata. I shot at that Miller, the guy you whupped. I got his horse. Lew, he burned that long, lean mountain man along the cheek, tryin' for a head shot. Actually this here Collins *hombre* was off to our left. None of us shot that way."

"You're sure about that?" Bannon demanded.

His mind was working swiftly. If one thing would arouse anger against Bishop among the settlers, it would be the killing of one of their own number, and particularly one so well liked as Collins had been.

Bannon stared at the rider. "Did you see anybody near him? Who was over at that side?"

"This here Collins *hombre* who got shot, he was in the front rank," Johnny said. "Then there was a heavy-set, sandy sort of guy with a beard and a tall *hombre* with a white hat and a dark coat."

The bearded man would be Lamport. The man in the white hat was Mort Harper.

Rock Bannon swung a leg over the saddle. "Johnny, you tell Red to sit tight," he said. "I'm riding to Poplar."

"Want me along?" Stark asked eagerly. "You better take some help. Those *hombres* are killin' now. They are in a sweat, all of them."

Rock shook his head. "No, I'll go it alone," he said. "Tell Red to wait at the cabin."

Rock wheeled the steel-dust and cut across the valley. There was still a chance to avoid a battle if he could get to Poplar in time, yet he had a feeling that Harper would not wait. Hostilities had begun, and that was what he had been playing for all the time. Now he had his excuse to wipe out the Bishop forces, and he would be quick to take advantage of it.

Before he was halfway down the valley, he reined in on the slope of a low hill. Miles to the south he could see a group of horsemen cutting across toward the line cabin. Bat Chavez was there alone with the wounded Murray.

Red would be starting soon, but would get there too late to help Bat or Murray. Within a matter of a half hour they would be attacking. From where he was, it would take him all of that time and probably more to reach them. There was no time to go back. Wheeling the steel-dust, he started down the valley, angling away from the group of riders.

In the distance around the peaks towering against the sky, dark clouds were banking. A jagged streak of lightning ripped the horizon to shreds of flame and then vanished, and there was a distant roll of thunder, muttering among the dark and distant ravines like the echoes of a far-away battle.

The gray horse ran through the tall grass, sweeping around groves of aspen and alder, keeping to the low ground. He splashed through a swale, crested a long low hill that cut athwart the valley, and turned at right angles down the draw toward the cover of the far-off trees. The cool wind whipped against his face, and he felt a breath of moist wind as it shifted, feeling for the course of the storm.

The big horse was running smoothly, liking the feel of running as he always did, letting his powerful muscles out and stretching them. Leaning forward to break the wind and let the weight of his body help the running horse, Rock Bannon talked to him, speaking softly to the stallion. He knew the stallion loved his voice, for between horse and man there was that companionship and understanding that come only when they have known many trails together, shared the water of the same creeks, and run over long swells of prairie as they were running now.

Then he heard the distant sound of a rifle, followed by a roll of shots.

"Bat, I hope to heaven you're under cover," he muttered. "I hope they didn't surprise you."

He eased the horse's running now because he might rush upon some of them sooner than he expected. He slid his rifle from the scabbard and raced into the trees. The sound of firing was nearer now. He slowed the horse to a walk, letting him take a blow, his eyes searching the brush. There was still some distance to go, but there was firing, and that meant that Bat was under cover. They had not caught him flat-footed at least.

He swung the horse up into the rocks and slid from the saddle, easing forward to the rim of the shelf overhanging the line cabin. Lying face down among the rocks, he could see puffs of smoke from the brush around the cabin. Waiting until he saw a gleam of light on a rifle, he fired.

Almost instantly a man some distance away leaped up and started to run for a boulder. Swinging his rifle, he snapped a shot at him, and the man went to his knees, and then started to crawl for shelter.

A rifle bellowed down below, and a shot glanced off a rock, kicking splinters into Bannon's face. He eased back and worked down the slope a bit, studying the situation below. One man was wounded, at least.

Suddenly a horseman leaped a horse from behind some trees and, dragging a flaming mass of brush, raced toward the cabin. It was a foolhardy thing to do, but instantly Bannon saw his purpose. The rifle fire had attracted Bat Chavez to the other side of the cabin. Rock lifted his own rifle and steadied it. A flashing instant of aim, and then he fired.

The horseman threw up his arms and toppled back off the horse, right into the mass of flaming brush. He screamed once, horribly, and then rolled clear, fighting the fire in his garments and dragging himself in the dust. Another man rushed from the brush to aid him, and Rock held his fire.

Suddenly there was a heavy roll of thunder. Looking around, he saw the clouds had come nearer, and now there was a sprinkle of rain. At the same instant he heard the pounding of horses' hoofs. Snapping a quick shot at the brush, he heard a startled yell. Then the attackers broke from the brush and, scrambling to their saddles, charged away across the valley. At that moment, the rain broke with a thundering roar, a veritable cloudburst.

Rushing to the steel-dust, he swung into the saddle. He put the animal around to a steep slide of shale and rode down to the barn near the corral. Johnny rushed up to him.

"You all right?"

"Yeah. How's Bat?"

"Don't know. Red went in. You go ahead. I'll fix your horse up."

Rock sprinted for the house and got in, slamming the door after him. Bat looked around, grinning widely.

"Man, was I glad to hear that rifle of yours," he said. "They had me surrounded. Lew wanted to get into it, but I was afraid his wound would open and start bleedin' again. Well, we drove 'em off."

"You get anybody?"

"Scratched a couple. Maybe got one. You got one that first shot. I seen him fall. That'll be one down and two bad hurt, maybe four. Looks like we come out of that on top."

"I was headed for Poplar and saw them comin'. I was afraid you'd be outside and they'd split up on you."

Chavez spat. "They mighty near did. I'd just been to the spring for water."

Rock stared into the fire. This would mean nothing one way or another. They had been turned back from the first attack, but they would not be convinced. He had killed a man. Who was it? That would matter a great deal, he knew. Certainly, if it was another of the settlers, he would have small chance of selling them on quitting.

Yet he was just as resolved now as before the attack. This thing must be stopped. It was never too late to try. The rain was roaring upon the roof. They would never expect him in a flood like that. They would be inside and expecting everyone else to be there, too. If he circled around and came down the cañon, it would be the best chance. If they were keeping watch at all, it would be from this direction. He would start in a few minutes. They were making coffee now. . . .

* * *

Sharon was outside when she saw the rain coming, and she waited for it, liking the cool air. Over the distant mountains across the valley, there were vivid streaks of lightning. It was already storming there, a frightful storm by all appearances.

She was alone and glad of it. Mary had wanted her to come to the Collins house, where several of the women had gathered, but she knew she could not stand to be cooped up now. She was restless, worried. Her father was out there, and, for all his courage and willingness to go, Tom Crockett was no fighting man. He was not like Bannon. Strangely now, she was but little worried about him. He was hard, seemingly impervious to harm.

Even now he might be over there across the valley. He might be killing her father, or her father might be shooting him. Twelve men had ridden away. Eight of them were settlers. Collins was dead and Dud Kitchen still too weak to ride, but the others had gone to a man. Mulholland, Satterfield, Pagones, Lamport, Purcell, Olsen, and Greene. And, of course, her father.

Then the rain came, a scattering of big drops, and then the rolling wall of it. She turned and went inside. There were a few places where the roof was not too tight. She put pans under them and lighted a light, which she put on the table near the window. Her father's leg was still not overly strong, and it worried her to think he was out there in all this.

She caught a glimpse of herself in the mirror, a tall, lovely girl with a great mass of red-gold hair done in two thick braids about her head, her face too pale, her eyes overly large.

She heard them coming before she saw them, and saw a horseman break away from the others and cross the grass, now worn thin from much travel. When the horse was stabled, he came in, stamping his feet and slipping out of his slicker. His gray hat was black with rain, and she took it close to the fire. The coffee was ready, and she poured a cup, and then went for a bowl to get some thick soup for him.

He sat down at the table, sat down suddenly, as if his legs had been cut off, and she noticed with a sudden qualm that he looked old, tired. His eyes lifted to hers and he smiled wanly.

"Guess I'm no fighting man, Sharon," he said. "I just wasn't cut out for it. When that man fell into the flames today, I nearly wilted."

"Who was it?" she asked quickly. "One of our men?"

"No, it was a teamster. One of the bunch that hangs around the saloon. His name was Osburn. We rushed the house, and one of the men inside opened fire. Wounded one of the men, first shot. We had the house surrounded, though, and would have had them in a few minutes. Then someone opened up on us from the cliff.

"It was Bannon, I'm sure of that. He killed Hy Miller. Got him with his first shot, although how he saw him I can't imagine. Then he wounded Satterfield. Shot him through the leg, about like I was. This Osburn got on a horse, and . . ." His voice rambled on, and all she could think about was that her father was home, that her father was safe.

After it all, when his voice had died away and he was eating the hot soup, she said: "And Bannon? Was he hurt?"

"No, he wasn't hurt. He never seems to get hurt. He's a hard man, Sharon."

"But a good man, Father!" she said suddenly. "He's a good man. Oh, I wish things were different."

"Don't think it, Sharon," her father said, shaking his head. "He's not for you. He's a wild, ruthless man, a man who lives by the gun. Collins is dead, and by one of this man's friends, and they'll never let up now, nor will we. It's a war to the end."

"But why, Father? Why?" Sharon's voice broke. "Oh, when I think that we might have gone by the other trail! We might have been in Oregon now. Sometimes I believe that everything Bannon ever said about Mort Harper is true. All we've done is to come on here into this trap, and now our oxen are gone, all but the two you use to plow, and we're in debt."

"I know." Crockett stirred restlessly. "But it might have been as bad wherever we went. You must understand that. We may be mistaken in Mort. He's done what he could, and he's standing by us in this fight."

The fire flickered and hissed with the falling drops of rain in the chimney, and Sharon crossed and knelt beside the fire, liking the warm feel of it on her knees. She sat there, staring into the flames, hearing the unrelenting thunder of the rain, and wondering where Rock Bannon was.

Where would it all end? That boy, Wes Freeman, slain in the hills. Then Collins, and now Miller. Dud Kitchen recovering from a wound. Jim Satterfield down, and the whole affair only beginning and no end in sight. The door opened suddenly and without warning, and she whirled, coming to her feet with her eyes wide.

Disappointment swept over her, and then fear. Pete Zapata was closing the door after him. He was smiling at her, his queer, flat face wet with rain, his narrow rattler's eyes searching the corners of the room.

"Not here?" he whispered hoarsely. "Pretty soon, maybe."

"Who . . . who do you mean?" she gasped.

Her father was sitting up very straight, his eyes on the man. Zapata glanced at him with thinly veiled contempt, and then shrugged.

"Who? That Rock Bannon. A few minutes ago he came down the cañon on his horse. Now he is here somewhere. Who knows? But soon he will come here, and when . . ." He smiled, showing his yellow teeth between thick lips. His eyes shifted from her to her father. "If one speaks to warn him, I'll kill the other one, you see?"

Fear left her lips stiff, her eyes wide. Slowly she turned back to the fire. Bannon would come here. Zapata was right. She knew he would come here. If Rock had come again to Poplar, he would not leave without seeing her. He might come at any minute.

She must think, she must somehow contrive to warn him—somehow!

The steel-dust liked the dim, shallow cave in which Rock stopped him, but he didn't like being left alone. He whimpered a little and made believe to snort with fear as Bannon started to move away, but when Rock spoke, the stallion quieted, resigned to what was to come.

Rock Bannon moved out swiftly, keeping under the trees but working his way closer and closer to the house of Pagones. He didn't know what he was getting into, but Pagones was the most reliable of them all, and the strongest one. If resistance to Harper was to come, it must come from him. Crockett lacked the force of character, even though he might have the will. Besides, Pagones knew that one of Harper's men had shot down Dud Kitchen.

Pagones hadn't chosen his potential son-in-law. Mary had done that for herself, but Pagones couldn't have found anyone he liked better. Dud was energetic, tireless, capable, and full of good humor. George Pagones, in his heart, had never felt sure of Mort Harper. He had listened with one part of his mind to Bannon's protests, even while the smooth words of Harper beguiled him.

Pagones had returned wet and tired. Like Crockett, he had no love of killing. He had seen Osburn tumble into the flames, and he had seen Miller killed. Knowing the trouble Miller had caused and how he had attacked Sharon while drunk, Pagones was not sorry to see him die. If it had to be someone, it might as well have been Miller. Yet seeing any man die is a shock, and he had been close to the man.

Many men are aggressive and willing enough to fight, but when they see death strike suddenly and horribly, their courage oozes away. Pagones had the courage to defend himself, but his heart was not in this fight, and the action of the day had served to make him very thoughtful.

Something was worrying Dud Kitchen. He had been noticing that for several days, yet there had been no chance to talk to him when the wom-enfolk were not around. He felt the need of talking to him now and got up and went into the room. He was there, beside the bed, when a breath of cold air struck him and he heard a startled gasp from his wife.

Gun in hand, he stepped back to the door. Rock Bannon was closing it after him. He turned now and looked at the gun in Pagones's hand. Bannon smiled grimly.

"Well, you've got the drop on me, Pag. What happens now?"

"What do you want here?" Pagones demanded sternly. "Don't you know if you keep coming back, they'll kill you?"

"Just so it isn't you, Pag," Bannon said. "I always reckoned you a friend."

Pagones holstered his gun. "Come in," he said. "I take it you've come to talk."

Mary and his wife stood facing him, their eyes shining with apprehension. There was a scuffling of feet from the other room, and Dud Kitchen was in the door.

"Howdy," he said. "They'll kill you, Rock. I heard Zapata say he was after you. He said he was going to get you next."

"All right." Rock dropped into a chair, his right-hand holster in his lap, the ivory gun butt near his right hand. His dark blue shirt was open at the neck, his leather jacket unbuttoned. The candle- and firelight flickered on the bright butts of the cartridges in his twin belts.

Dud's face was very pale, but somehow Rock sensed that Dud was glad to see him, and it made him feel better and made the talk come easier. Pagones's cheekbones glistened in the firelight, and his eyes were steady on Bannon's face as he waited for him to begin. It was very still in the room. A drop of water fell into the fire and hissed itself into extinction.

Mary Pagones stooped, her freckles dark against the pallor of her face, and dropped a handful of small sticks on the fire.

"Pag," Bannon began slowly, "I've never wanted this fight. I don't think you have. I don't think Crockett did, either, or Dud here. There's no use me tryin' to talk to Tom. He's a good man and he knows what he wants, but he hasn't force enough to make it stick. He couldn't stand against Harper. There's only one man here can do that, Pagones, and that's you."

"Harper's my friend," Pagones said evenly. "He led us here. This is his fight and ours."

"You don't believe that," Rock said. "Not down inside, you don't. Collins's death brought you into it. That made it your fight and Crockett's fight.

The truth is, all you men want is homes. That's what your wife wants, and Mary. That's what Sharon wants, too. That's what Cap wants, and the rest of them.

"What Mort Harper wants is land and power. He intends to have them, no matter who dies or when. I've been here before to try to stop this trouble. I'm here again now.

"One of our men died first, and he was a good boy. He was murdered, Pagones, murdered like no man in the wagon train would kill any man. Purcell didn't like me. Neither did Lamport. Cap was your leader, but he listened too quick to that glib tongue of Harper's."

"We all did," Dud said. "I listened, too. I listened for a while, anyway." Mary moved up behind his chair and put her hand on his shoulder. He looked up quickly, and she smiled.

"Get to the point!" Pagones said. All that Bannon said was true. He knew it as well as Rock. He had listened to Harper, but secretly he had always been afraid that Bannon was right. He had been afraid of this trail. They had no oxen now, and they had no money. They were here, and they could not escape.

Rock leaned a hand on his knee. "Pagones, my boys say they didn't kill Collins."

CHAPTER SEVEN

Dud Kitchen drew in his breath, and Mary looked at him in sudden apprehension.

"What's that you say?" Pagones demanded.

"I repeat. I talked to my boys, and they say they didn't kill Collins. Bat Chavez couldn't see anything, but Zapata, Stark, and Murray weren't even facing toward Collins then. They say they didn't kill him."

"There was a lot of shooting," Pagones said. "Anything might've happened."

"That's right," Bannon agreed. "But my boys don't think they shot Collins, and that leaves a big question."

"It don't leave no question for me!" Dud flared suddenly. "I saw that wound of Collins's! And he was shot in the back!"

Pagones's face hardened. He stared down at the floor, his jaw muscles working. Was nothing ever simple anymore? Was there nothing on which a man could depend? How had he got into this mess, anyway? What should he do?

"Who do you think?" he asked. "You mean Zapata?"

Their eyes were all on Rock Bannon, waiting, tense. "No," he said. "I mean Mort Harper."

"But, man, that's crazy!" Pagones leaped to his feet. "What would be the object? Is there any reason why he would kill a man on his own side?"

"You know the answer to that as well as I," Bannon said. He got up, too. "He wanted you in this fight, and that was the only way he could get you. Purcell and Lamport were fire-eaters. They were in, but they weren't enough. He wanted the rest of you, the good, sober, industrious citizens, the men whose reputations at home were good, the men who would look honest to the military if they ever came West."

"I saw that wound," Kitchen repeated. "Collins was killed with a small gun, a small gun with flat-nose or split-ended bullets."

"Who has such a gun?" Pagones said. "You all know that Harper carries a Dragoon, like the rest of us."

"In sight, he does," Bannon agreed. "Mort Harper may pack another one." He stopped, feet wide apart. "I've got to get out of here, Pag. I've got to get going and fast. There's not much chance of anybody being out tonight, but I can't gamble on that. I've got to get away from here, and this is the last time I'll come. I've tried to tell you about Mort Harper for a long time. You've got your last chance to break away, because I'm telling you flat. If you don't break away, there won't be a building standing on this ground within forty-eight hours."

Pagones's head jerked up. "Is that an ultimatum?"

"You bet it is!" Bannon snapped. "If I'd let Bishop have his head, you'd have all been out of here long ago. Wes would be alive now, and Collins, and Murray wouldn't be packin' that slug in his leg, and Dud would be on his feet. If I'd not kept Bishop off you, he would have faced you with forty armed men and ordered you off before you had a stake down or a foundation laid.

"Those boys of ours are spoilin' for a fight. They hate Harper's innards, and they want Zapata. He's a murderin' outlaw, and they all know it."

"I don't know that I can do anything," Pagones protested. "We have to think of Zapata as it is. Harper's the only thing that keeps him and those teamsters off our places and away from our women, anyway!"

Rock Bannon started for the door. With his hand on the latch, he turned, sliding into his slicker.

"You step aside and there won't be any Zapata or his friends," he declared. "We'll wipe them out so fast they'll only be a memory. We just don't want to kill good people. You can keep your places. We let you come in, and we'll let you stay."

He turned and slipped out the door into the rain. For an instant, he hesitated, letting his eyes grow accustomed to the dark. Rain fell in slanting sheets, striking his face like hail stones and rattling against his oilskin slicker like on a tin roof. Water stood in puddles on the ground, and, when he stepped down, a large drop fell from a tree down the back of his neck.

He hesitated, close against the wet tree trunk, and stared into the night. There was a glow of light from the window of the Crockett place. Somebody was still up. He hesitated, knowing it was dangerous to remain longer, yet longing for a sight of Sharon, for the chance to take her in his arms.

He never had. He had never kissed her, never held her hand. It was all a matter of their eyes, and yet he felt she understood and, perhaps, responded a little to his feeling.

There were lights from the saloon. They would all be down there now, playing cards, drinking. It was a pity he had none of the boys here. They could go in and wipe them out in one final, desperate battle. Lightning flashed and revealed the stark wet outlines of the buildings, the green of the grass, worn down now, between him and the Crockett cabin.

He stepped out from the tree and started across the open, hearing the far-off thunder muttering among the peaks of the mountains beyond the valley, muttering among the cliffs and boulders like a disgruntled man in his sleep.

He did not fasten his slicker, but held it together with his left hand and kept his right in his pocket, slopping across the wet ground with the rain battering the brim of his hat, beating with angry, skeleton fingers against the slicker.

Under the trees, he hesitated, watching the house. There was no horse around. Suddenly a column of sparks went up from the chimney, as if someone had thrown some sticks on the fire. He started to move, and another cluster of sparks went up. He hesitated. A signal? But who would know he was near?

A third time. Three times was a warning, three smokes, three rifle shots—what could it be? Who could know he was here? It was nonsense, of course, but the sparks made him feel uneasy.

Then, again, three times, once very weakly, sparks mounted from the chimney. Somebody was playing with the fire, tapping with a stick on the burning wood or stirring the fire.

No matter. He was going in. He felt cold, and the warmth of the room would be good again before he began his long ride to the line cabin. A long ride, because it would be foolhardy to go down the cañon toward the valley.

He stepped out from under the tree and walked up to the house. His boots made sucking noises in the mud before the door. Lightning flashed and water glistened on the smooth boards of the door. He should knock, but he stepped up and, keeping to the left of the door, reached across with his left hand and drew the door wide.

A gun blasted, and he saw the sudden dart of fire from the darkness by the fireplace. The bullet smashed into the door, and then he went in with a rush.

He caught a glimpse of Sharon, her eyes wide with fright, scrambling away from the fire. Zapata lunged from the shadows, his face set in a snarl of bared teeth and gleaming eyes. His gun blasted again, and a bullet snatched at Rock's jacket. Bannon thumbed his gun.

Zapata staggered, as though struck by a blow in the stomach. As Rock started for him, he leaped for an inner door. Rock lunged after him, firing again. There was a crash as Zapata went through a sack-covered window.

Wheeling, Rock leaped for the door and went out. Zapata's gun barked, and something laid a white-hot iron across his leg. Rock brought his gun up, turned his right side to the crouching man, and fired again, fired as though on a target range.

Zapata coughed, and his pistol dropped into the mud. He clawed with agonized fingers at his other gun, and Rock Bannon could see the front of his shirt darkening with the pounding rain and with blood. Then Bannon fired again, and Zapata went down, clawing at the mud.

A door slammed, and there was a yell. Rock wheeled and saw Sharon in the doorway. "I can't stop," he said. "Talk to Pagones." And even as he spoke, he was running across the worn grass toward the trees.

A rifle barked and then another, then there were intermittent shots. Crying with fear for him, Sharon Crockett stood in the door, staring into the darkness. Lightning flared, and through the slanting rain she caught a brief glimpse of him. A rifle flared, and then he was gone into the trees. A moment later, they heard the pounding of hoofs.

"They'll never catch him on that horse," Tom Crockett said. "He got away!"

Sharon turned, and her father was smiling.

"Yes, Daughter, I'm glad he got away. I'm glad he killed that murderer."

"Oh, Father!" Then his arms were around her, and, as running feet slapped in the mud outside, he pushed the door shut. "He'll get away!" she cried. "He must get away."

The door slammed open, and Mort Harper shoved into the room. Behind him were four men, their faces hard, their guns ready.

"What was he doing here?" Harper demanded. "That man's a killer! He's our enemy. Why should he come here?"

"I don't know why he came," Crockett said coldly. "He never had a chance to say. Zapata had been waiting for him all evening. He seemed to believe he would be here. When Bannon came in, he fired and missed. He won't miss again."

Harper stared at him, his face livid and angry under the glistening dampness of the rain.

"You seem glad!" he cried.

"I am!" Crockett said. "Yes, I'm glad! That Zapata was a killer, and he deserved killing."

"And I'm glad," Sharon said, her chin lifted. "I'm glad Bannon killed him, glad that Bannon got away."

There was an angry mutter from the men behind Harper, but Mort put up a restraining hand. "So? This sounds like rebellion. Well, we'll have none of that in this camp. I've been patient with you people, and especially patient with you, Sharon, but my patience is wearing thin."

"Who cares about your patience?" Anger rose in

Sharon's eyes. "Your soft talk and lies won't convince us any longer. We want our oxen back tomorrow. We've had enough of this. We'll get out of here tomorrow if we have to walk."

"Let's teach 'em a lesson, boss," one man said angrily. "To blazes with this palaver!"

"Not now," Harper said. His nostrils were flared with anger, and his face was hard. "Later!"

When the door closed after them, Tom Crockett's face was white. "Well, Sharon," he said quietly, "for better or worse, there it is. Tomorrow we may have to fight. Your mother helped me fight Indians once, long ago. Could you?"

Sharon turned, and suddenly she smiled. "Do you need to ask?"

"No." He smiled back, and she could see a new light in his eyes, almost as if the killing of Zapata and the statement to Harper had made him younger, stronger. "No, I don't," he repeated. "You'd better get some sleep. I'm going to clean my rifle."

Rock Bannon's steel-dust took the trail up the cañon at a rapid clip. They might follow him, Bannon knew, and he needed all the lead he could get. Some of those men had been in these hills for quite some time, yet if he could get away into the wilderness around Day's River, they would never find him.

Shooting it out with six or seven desperate killers was no part of his plan, and he knew the teamsters who had come to Poplar were just that, a band of renegades recruited from the scourings of the wagon trains passing through the fort. After the immediate dash, however, he slowed down to give the steel-dust better footing.

He turned northeast when he came out of Poplar Cañon and rode down into a deep draw that ended in a meadow. The bottom of the draw was roaring with water that had run off the mountains, but as yet it was no more than a foot deep. Far below, he could hear the thunder of Day's River, roaring at full flood now.

The cañon through the narrows would be a ghastly sight with its weight of thundering white water. Always a turmoil, now it would be doubled and tripled by the cloudburst. Rain slanted down, pouring unceasingly on the hills.

The trail by which he had come would be useless on his return. By now the water would be too deep in the narrow cañon up which he had ridden. He must find a new trail, a way to cut back from the primitive wilderness into which he was riding and down through the valley where Freeman had been killed, and then through the mountains.

Briefly he halted the big stallion in the lee of a jutting shoulder of granite where wind and rain were cast off into the flat of the valley. Knowing his horse would need every ounce of strength, he swung down. His shoulder against the rock, he studied the situation in his mind's eye.

His first desperate flight had taken him northeast into the wild country. Had he headed south he must soon have come out on the plains beyond the entrance to Bishop's Valley, where he would have nothing but the speed of his own horse to assist his escape.

He was needed here, now. Any flight was temporary, so in turning north he had kept himself within striking distance of the enemy. His problem now was to find a way through the rugged mountain barrier, towering thousands of feet above him, into Bishop's Valley, and across the valley to home.

No man knew these mountains well, but Hardy Bishop best of all. Next to him, Rock himself knew them best, but with all his knowledge they presented a weird tangle of ridges, cañons, jagged crests, peaks, and chasms. At the upper end of the valley, the stream roared down a gorge often 3,000 feet deep and with only the thinnest of trails along the cliffs of the narrows.

The isolated valley might have been walled for the express purpose of keeping him out, for as he ran over the possible routes into the valley, one by one he had to reject them. Bailey's Creek would be a thundering torrent now, water roaring eight to ten feet deep in the narrow cañon. Trapper's Gulch would be no better, and the only other two routes would be equally impassable.

Rock stared at the dark bulk of the mountain through the slanting rain. He stared at it, but could see nothing but Stygian darkness. Every branch, every rivulet, and every stream would be a roaring cataract now. If there was a route into the valley now, it must be over the ridge. The very thought made him swallow and turn chill. He knew what those ridges and peaks were in quiet hours. They could be traveled, and he had traveled them, but only when he could see and feel his way along. Now, with lightning crashing, with thunder butting against the cliffs, and with clouds gathered around them, it would be an awful inferno of lightning and granite, a place for no living thing.

Yet, the thought in the back of his mind kept returning. Hardy Bishop was alone, or practically so. He had sent Red to the line cabin nearest Harper with most of the fighting men. Others were in a cabin near the narrows, miles away. Only two men would be at home aside from the cook.

Rock Bannon did not make the mistake of underestimating his enemy. Mort Harper had planned this foray with care. He would not have begun without a careful study of the forces to be arrayed against him. He would know how many men were at the line cabin, and the result of his figuring must certainly be to convince him that the ranch house was unprotected, and Hardy Bishop, the heart, soul, and brain of the Bishop empire, was there.

There was a route over the mountain. Once, by day, Bannon had traveled it. He must skirt a cañon hundreds of feet deep along a path that clung like an eyebrow to the sheer face of the cliff. He must ride across the long swelling slope of the mountain among trees and boulders, and then between two peaks, and angle through the forest down the opposite side.

At best, it was a twelve-mile ride, and might stretch that a bit. Even by day it was dangerous and slow going. And he needed only his own eyes to convince him that lightning was making a playground of the hillside now.

"All right, boy," he said gently to the horse. "You aren't going to like this, but neither am I." He swung into the saddle and moved out into the wind.

As he breasted the shoulder of granite, the wind struck him like a solid wall, and the rain lashed at his garments, plucking at the fastenings of his oilskin. He turned the horse down the cañon that would take them to the cliff face across which he must ride. He preferred not to think of that.

As he drew near, the cañon walls began to close in upon him, until it became a giant chute down which the water thundered in a mighty Niagara of sound. Great masses of water churned in an enormous maelstrom below and the steel-dust snorted and shied from its roaring.

Rock spoke to the horse and touched him on the shoulder. Reassured, he felt gingerly for the path and moved out. A spout of water gushing from some crack in the rock struck Rock like a blow, drenching him anew and making the stallion jump. He steadied the horse with a tight rein, and then relaxed and let the horse have his head. He could see absolutely nothing ahead of him.

Thunder and the rolling of gigantic boulders reverberated down the rock-walled cañon, and occasional lightning-lit flares showed him glimpses of a weird nightmare of glistening rock and tumbling white water that caught the flame and hurled it in millions of tiny shafts on down the cañon.

The steel-dust walked steadily, facing the wind but with bowed head, hesitating only occasionally to feel its way around some great rock or sudden, unexpected heap of debris.

The hoarse wind howled down the channel of rock, turning its shouting to a weird scream on corners where the pines feathered down into the passage of the wind. Battered by rain and wind, Rock Bannon bent his head and rode on, beaten, soaked, bedraggled, with no eyes to see, only trusting to the sure-footed mountain horse and its blind instinct.

Once, when the lightning lifted the whole scene into stark relief, he glimpsed a sight that would not leave him if he lived to be one hundred. For one brief, all-encompassing moment he saw the cañon as he never wanted to see it again.

The stallion had reached a bend and for a moment hesitated to relax its straining, careful muscles. In that instant, the lightning flared.

Before them, the cañon dropped steeply away, like the walls of a gigantic stairway, black, glistening walls slanted by the steel of driving rain, cut by volleys of hail, and accompanied by the roar of the cataract below.

The white water roared 200 feet down, and banked in a cul-de-sac in the rock was a piled-up mass of foam, fifteen or twenty feet high, bulging and glistening. At each instant, wind or water ripped some of it away and shot it, churning, down the fury of raging water below. Thunder roared a salvo, and the echoes responded, and a wild cliff-clinging cedar threshed madly in the wind, as if to tear free its roots and blow away to some place of relief from the storm.

Lightning crackled, and thunder drummed against the cliffs, and the scene blacked out suddenly into abysmal darkness. The steel-dust moved on, rounding the point of the rock and starting to climb. Then, as if by a miracle, they were out of the cañon, but turning up a narrow crevice in the rock with water rushing, inches deep, beneath the stallion's hoofs. A misstep here and they would tumble down the crevice and pitch off into the awful blackness above the water. But the stallion was sure-footed, and suddenly they came out on the swell of the mountain slope.

The lightning below was nothing to this. Here darkness was a series of fleeting intervals shot through with thunderbolts, and each jagged streak lighted the night like a blaze from Hades. Gaunt shoulders of the mountain butted against the bulging weight of cloud, and the skeleton fingers of long-dead pines felt stiffly of the wind.

Stunned by the storm, the stallion plodded on, and Rock swayed in the saddle, buffeted and hammered, as they walked across that bare, dead slope among the boulders, pushing relentlessly, tirelessly against the massive wall of the wind. A flash of lightning, and a tree ahead detonated like a shell, and bits of it flew off into space with the wild complaining of a ricocheted bullet. The stub of the tree smoked, sputtered with flame, and went out, leaving a vague smell of charred wood and brimstone.

A long time later, dawn felt its way over the mountains beyond and behind him, and the darkness turned gray, and then rose and flame climbed the peaks. Rock rode on, sullen, beaten, overburdened with weariness. The high cliffs behind him turned their rust-colored heights to jagged bursts of frozen flame, but he did not notice. Weary, the stallion plodded down the last mile of slope and into the rain-flattened grass of the plain.

The valley was empty. Rock lifted his red-rimmed eyes and stared south. He saw no horsemen, no movement. He had beaten them. He would be home before they came. And once he was home, he could stand beside the big old man who called him son, and they would face the world together, if need be.

Let Harper come. He would learn what fighting meant. These men were not of the same flesh or the same blood, but the response within them was the same, and the fire that shaped the steel of their natures was the same. They were men bred to the Colt. Bred to the law of strength. Men who knew justice, but could fight to defend what was theirs and what they believed.

He was not thinking that. He was thinking nothing. He was only moving. The steel-dust plodded on into the ranch yard, and he fell rather than stepped from the saddle. Springer rushed out to get his horse.

"My stars, man! How'd you get here?"

"Over the mountain," Bannon said, and walked toward the house.

Awed, Springer turned and looked toward the towering, 6,000-foot ridge. "Over the mountain," he said. "Over the mountain!" He stripped the saddle from the big horse and turned it into the corral, and then almost ran to the bunkhouse to tell Turner. "Over the mountain!"

Hardy Bishop looked up from his great chair, and his eyes sharpened. Rock raised a hand, and then walked on through the room, stripping his sodden clothing as he went. When he reached the bed, he pulled off one boot and then rolled over and stretched out, his left spur digging into the blanket.

Bishop followed him to the room and stared down at him grimly, then he walked back and dropped into the chair. Well, he reflected, for that he could be thankful. He had a man for a son.

It was a long time ago that he first came into this valley with old John Day. They had come down through the narrows and looked out over the wide, beautiful length of it, and he had seen what he knew he was looking for. He had seen paradise.

There were men in the West then, men who roamed the streams for beaver or the plains for buffalo. They lived and traded and fought with the Indians, learning their ways and going them one better. They pushed on into new country, country no white man had seen.

There were men like John Coulter, who first looked into the Yellowstone region, old Jim Bridger, who knew the West as few men. There were John Day, Smith, Hoback, Wilson Price Hunt, Kit Carson, and Robert Stuart. Most of them came for fur or game, and later they came for gold, but there were a few even then who looked for homes, and of the first was Hardy Bishop.

He had settled here, buying the land from the Indians and trading with them long before any other white man dwelled in the region. Once a whole year had passed when he saw not even a trapper.

The Kaws were usually his friends, but the Crows were not, and occasionally raiding parties of Blackfeet came down from the north. When they were friendly, he talked or traded, and, when they wanted to fight, he fought. After a while, even the Crows left him alone, learning friendship was more profitable than death, and many had died.

Bad days were coming. From the seat in the great hide-bound chair, Hardy Bishop could see that. The trouble with Indians would be nothing to the trouble with white men, and he was glad that Rock was a man who put peace first, but who handled a gun fast.

He raised his great head, his eyes twinkling. They were keen eyes that could see far and well. Even the Indians respected them. He could, they said, trail a snake across a flat rock, or a duck downstream through rough water. What he saw now was a horseman, riding toward the ranch. One lone horseman, and there was something odd in the way he rode.

It was not a man. It was a woman. A white woman. Hardy Bishop heaved himself ponderously from the chair. It had been almost ten years since he had seen a white woman! He walked slowly to the door, hitching his guns around just in case.

The sun caught her hair and turned it to living flame. His dark eyes kindled. She rode up to the steps, and he saw Springer and Turner in the bunkhouse door, gaping. She swung down from her black mare and walked over to him. She was wearing trousers and a man's shirt. Her throat was bare in the open neck. He smiled. Here was a woman!

Chapter Eight

Sharon looked up at Bishop, astonished. Somehow, she had always known he would be big, but not such a monster of a man. Six feet four he stood, in his socks, and weighing 300 pounds. His head was covered with a shock of iron-gray hair, in tight curls. His eyes twinkled, and massive forearms and hands jutted from his sleeves.

"Come in! Come in!" he boomed. "You'll be Sharon Crockett, then. I've heard of you. Heard a sight of you!" He looked around as she hesitated on the steps. "What's the matter? Not afraid of an old man, are you? Come in."

"It isn't that. Only we've come here like this . . . and it was your land, and . . ."

"Don't explain." He shook his head. "Come in and sit down. You're the first white woman who ever walked into this house. First one ever saw it, I reckon. Rock, he's asleep. Dead to the world."

"He's safe then?" she asked. "I was afraid. I saw them go after him."

"There was trouble?" He looked at her keenly. "What happened?"

She told him about the killing of Pete Zapata and what had happened afterward. "That's why I'm here," she said. "In a way, I'm asking for peace. We didn't know. We were foolish not to have listened to Rock in the beginning, when he told us about Mort. My father and the settlers want peace. I don't know about Pike Purcell and Lamport, but I can speak for the rest of us."

Bishop nodded his head. "Rock told me what he was goin' for. So he killed Zapata? That'll please the boys." He turned his head. "Dave!" he bellowed.

A face covered with a shock of mussed hair and beard shoved into the door.

"Bring us some coffee! And some of that cake! We've got a lady here, by . . ." He flushed. "Excuse me, ma'am. Reckon my manners need a goin' over. We cuss a sight around here. A sight too much, I reckon. 'Course, I ain't never figured on gettin' into heaven, anyways. I been pretty much of a sinner and not much of a repenter. Reckon they'd have to widen the gate some. I'd be a sight of weight to get into heaven. Most likely, they'd have to put some cribbin' under the cloud I set on, too." He chuckled, looking at her. "So you're the girl what's goin' to marry Rock?"

She jumped and flushed. "Why! Why, I . . ."

"Don't let it get you down, ma'am. Reckon I'm a blunt old codger. It's true enough, the boy ain't said a word to me about it, but I can see what's in his eyes. I ain't raised the lad for nothin'. When he took off on this rampage, I was hopin' he'd find himself a gal. You like him, ma'am?" He looked at her sharply, his eyes filled with humor. "You goin' to marry him?"

"Why, I don't know," she protested. "I don't know that he wants me."

"Now, listen here. Don't you go givin' me any of that demure, folded-hands palaver. That may go for those young bucks, but not for me. You know as well as I do, if a woman sets her cap for a man, he ain't got a chance. Only if he runs. That's all. Either give up and marry the gal or get clean out of the country and don't leave no address behind. Nor no trail sign, neither.

"You might fool some young sprout with that 'he hasn't asked me' business, but not me. I seen many a young buck Indian give twenty head of ponies for some squaw when he could have had better ones for ten. Just because she wanted him like and caused him to figure the price was cheap.

"No, sir. I'd rather try to get away from a bear trap on each foot and each hand than a woman with her head set on marriage."

Flushed with embarrassment, she ignored what he had said.

"Then . . . then, you'll let us have peace, sir? You won't be fighting us if we draw off from Harper?"

"Of course not, ma'am. I reckon it'd be a right nice thing to have a few folks around once in a while." His eyes flashed. "But no more, you understand. Only this bunch of yours. No more!"

"And we can have our land, then?" she persisted.

"Sure, you can have it. You can have what them other fellers got, too, when they get out. Sure, you can have it. I can't set my hand to paper on it, though, because I never did learn to write. That's true, ma'am. Never learned to write, nor to read. But I can put my name on the side of a house with a six-shooter. I can do that. But them pens. They always figured to be a sight too small for my hands. No, I can't read printin', but I can read sign. I trailed a Blackfoot what stole a horse from me clean to Montana one time. Trailed him six hundred miles, believe me or not. Yes, ma'am, I come back with the horse and his scalp. Took it right in his own village."

A startled yell rang out, and Springer burst through the door.

"Boss! Boss! Here they come! Oh, quick, man! Here they . . . !"

His voice died in the report of a gun, and Hardy Bishop lunged from his chair to see men charging the porch.

Turner had started from the bunkhouse, but the rush of the horses rode him down. They heard his wild, agonized screams as he went down under the pounding hoofs. Sharon never saw the old man reach for his guns, but suddenly they were spouting flame. She saw a man stagger back from the door clutching at his breast, blood pouring over his hand.

Then a wild figure wearing one boot appeared from the other room, swinging gun belts about his hips. Then Rock Bannon, too, was firing.

A sound came at a rear window, and he turned and fired from the hip. A dark form looming there vanished. The attack broke, and Rock Bannon rushed to the rifle rack and jerked down two Henry rifles. Then he ran back, thrusting one at Bishop.

The old man dropped to his knees beside a window.

"Come up on us fast," he said. "I was talkin' to this gal." Rock's eyes swung to her, and then amazement faded to sudden grimness. With horror, she saw suspicion mount in his eyes.

A wild chorus of yells sounded from outside, and then a volley of shots smashed through the windows. The lamp scattered in a thousand pieces, and from the kitchen they heard a cursing, and then the crash of a buffalo gun.

"How many did you see?" Rock demanded.

"Most like a dozen," Bishop said. "We got two or three that first rush."

"A dozen?" He wheeled to the girl. "Did the settlers come? Did they? Are they fighting us now?"

"Can't be that," Bishop said, staring out at the ranch yard, his eyes probing the corral. "No chance of that. This girl come with peace talk."

"And while she was talking, they rode in on us!" Rock raged.

Sharon came up, her eyes wide. "Oh, you can't believe that! You can't! I . . ."

The *thud* of bullets into the logs of the house drowned her voice, along with the crashing of guns. Rock Bannon was slipping from window to window, moving on his feet like an Indian. He had yanked off his other boot now. A shot smashed the water *olla* that hung near the door. Bannon fired, and a man toppled from behind the corner of the corral and sprawled on the hard-packed ground near the body of Turner.

"They're goin' to rush us," Bannon said suddenly. He began loading his Colts. "Get set, Hardy. They are goin' to rush."

"Let 'em come! The sneak-thievin', pelt-robbin', trap-lootin' scum! Let 'em come! More'll come than'll go back!" As the outlaws rushed suddenly, charging in a scattered line, the old man burst through the door, his Colt smoking. A man screamed and grabbed his middle and took three staggering steps, and then sprawled his full length on the ground. Another man went down, and then a gun bellowed and the old man winced, took another step, and then toppled back into the room.

Sharon stared at him in horror, and then ran to him. He looked shocked.

"Hit me! They hit me! Give me my gun, ma'am. I'll kill the scum like the trap-robbin' wolverines they are!"

"*Ssh,* be still," she whispered. She began tearing the shirt away from the massive chest to search for the wound.

Steadily, using now one gun and then the other, Rock Bannon fired. He could sense uncertainty among the attackers. They had shot the old man, but four of their own number were down, and probably others were wounded. They were beginning to lose all desire for battle.

Watching closely, Rock saw a flicker of movement behind a corral trough. He watched, lifted his rifle, and took careful aim, and, when the movement came again, he fired, just under the trough.

A yell rang out, and he saw a man lift up to his full height, and then topple over.

"All right!" Bannon shouted. "Come on and get me! You wanted me! But you'd better come before the boys get in from north camp, or they'll spoil my fun."

They wouldn't believe him, but it might make them doubtful. He heard voices raised in argument. Then there was silence. He reloaded all the guns, his own, Bishop's Henry, and the old man's six-guns. It was mid-afternoon, and the sun was hot. If they waited until night, he was going to have a bad time of it.

There was a chance, however, that they would believe his story or fear that someone from the line cabin might ride far enough this way to hear the shots. If both groups came, they would be caught between two fires and wiped out. An hour passed, and there was no sound.

"Rock." Sharon was standing behind him. "We'd better get him on a bed."

He avoided her eyes, but got up and put down his rifle. It was a struggle, but they lifted Bishop off the floor and put him on his homemade four-poster. While Sharon bent over him, bathing the wound and treating it as best she could, Rock walked back to the windows.

Like a caged panther, he prowled from window to window. Outside, all was still. Only the bodies of the dead lay on the hard-packed ground of the ranch yard. A dust devil started somewhere on the plain and twisted in the grass of the meadow, and then skipped across the ranch yard, stirring around the body of Turner and blowing in his hair.

Turner was dead. The old man had been with them almost as long as Rock himself. He had been like one of the family. And Bob Springer was gone, blasted from life suddenly and all the young man's enthusiastic plans for a ranch of his own. Well, they would pay. They would pay to the last man.

The steel-dust had come back from the end of the corral near the creek. He seemed curious and approached the body lying near the trough with delicate hoofs, ready to shy. He snuffed at the body, caught the scent of blood, and jerked away, eyes distended and nostrils wide.

There was no one in sight. Apparently the attackers had drawn off. They had anticipated no such defense as this. They had had no idea that Rock Bannon was home, nor had they realized what a fighter the old man could be. They had to learn what the Crows had learned long since.

Rock waited another hour, continuing his slow prowl. Within the house he was comparatively safe, and he knew that to go out before he was sure was to tempt fate. From time to time he went into the bedroom where Bishop lay on the four-poster. He was unconscious or asleep, Sharon sitting beside him.

He avoided her eyes, yet the thought kept returning, filling him with bitterness, that she had ridden here with peace talk and that under cover of her talk Harper's men had made their approach. Knowing Bishop, he knew that unless his attention had been diverted, no rider or group of riders could have reached the ranch without being seen.

Had she planned with Mort Harper to do this thing? Everything he knew about the girl compelled him to believe she would do nothing of the kind, yet the thought persisted; it was almost too much of a coincidence.

After all, what reason had he to believe otherwise? Hadn't she admired Harper? Hadn't Pete Zapata been waiting in her cabin for him? Perhaps she had tried to warn him by throwing sticks on the fire, or it could have been an accident. The fact remained that, while visiting her, he had almost been killed in a trap laid by Zapata, and, while she had been making peace talk with Bishop, the raiding party had struck. It was not her fault they were not dead, both of them.

He knew she came to the door from time to time, and once she started to speak, but then turned away as he avoided her eyes.

Rock was crouching by a window when the sound of horse's hoofs brought him to his feet. It was Bat Chavez astride a slim, fast buckskin. The horse shied violently at Turner's body, and Bat had a hard time getting him to the door.

Bannon rushed out. "Everything all right at the line cabin?"

"Shucks, man!" Bat exploded. "That's what I was goin' to ask you. What happened here?"

"They hit us. Dave opened up from the kitchen.

Hardy and I shot it out up here. Bishop's down, hit pretty bad. They got Springer and Turner, as you can see."

"Saw them cuttin' across the valley for Poplar a few minutes ago. The boys are gettin' restless, Rock. They want to ride over and wind this up."

"No more than I do," Bannon said shortly. "Yes, we're goin'. We'll ride over and wipe that place out."

"Oh, no, you mustn't." Sharon had come into the door behind Rock. "Please, Rock. You mustn't. The settlers don't want to fight any more. It's just Harper's crowd."

"Maybe that's true," Bannon said, "but I've seen no sign of them quittin' yet. There were at least twelve men in this bunch. Did Harper have twelve men of his own? Not that I saw, he didn't. And Zapata's dead. So's Miller. Where would he get twelve men?"

He turned back to Chavez. "Get some food into you, Bat, and then ride back. I'll be down before long, and, when I am, we'll cross that valley. If the settlers get in the way, they'll get what the rest of them got . . . what they gave Turner and Springer here! We've dallied long enough."

Rock Bannon turned and walked back into the house. Sharon stared at him, her face white.

"Then you won't believe me?" she protested. "You'll go over there and kill innocent people?"

"Who killed Springer and Turner?" Rock demanded harshly. "In what way had they offended? I don't know that your settlers are innocent. I tried to tell them what they were going into, and they wouldn't believe me. Well, they came, and, if they get their tails in a crack, they've only themselves to blame.

"I argued with them. I argued with Bishop to give them a break, and now this happens. There were twelve men in that attack on us. At least twelve! Well, some of them died out there, but you and I both know that Harper didn't have twelve men. Perhaps eight, at best. They came in here and killed two of our boys and wounded Bishop. That old man in there has been a father to me. He's been more than most fathers. He's been a guide and a teacher, and all I know I learned from him. He may die, and, if he does, the fault was mine for ever letting this bunch of squatters in here."

The girl clasped her hands in distress. "Please, Rock!" she protested. "You can't do this. Most of your men don't know one from the other. The settlers would be killed whether they fought or not. Their homes will be burned."

"If they don't fight, they won't be hurt," he insisted stubbornly. "Next time that Harper attacks, he might get us all. Anyway, it looks to me like they were plenty willing to ride in on Harper's coattails and get all they could while the getting was easy."

"That's not true," she protested hotly. "They wanted to do the right thing. They thought they were doing the right thing. They believed Harper was honest."

Rock slid into his buckskin coat and picked up his hat. His face was grim and hard. He could not look at Sharon. He knew if their eyes ever met it would tear the heart out of him. Yet he also knew he had waited too long now, that if he had resorted to guns long ago, so many things might not have happened. Springer might be living, and Turner, and Collins, the settler. He started for the door, picking up his rifle from where he had left it.

"Rock," Sharon said, "if you go back, I will, too. The first one of your men who puts a hand on a settler's home, I'll kill with my own rifle."

For the first time he looked at her, and her eyes were flashing with pain and anger. "Go, then!" he said brutally. "But if you're half as smart as I think you are, you'll take your friends and head for the hills. Go! I'll give you a start. Warn Harper, too, if you want. Let him know we're coming. But if you want to save that precious pack of settlers, get them out of Poplar. Take to the hills until this is over . . . but be out of town before my boys ride in."

He walked to the door and went out. She saw him stop by the corral and pick up a rope, and then go to the corral for the steel-dust. Running from the house, she threw herself into the saddle of her own black mare, which had been tied at the corner of the house. Spurring her to top speed, she sprang out on the long ride across the valley.

Rock Bannon did not look up or turn his head, but in his heart and mind the hard hoofs pounded like the pulse in his veins, pounded harder and harder, and then vanished with the dying sound of the running horse.

He saddled the steel-dust, and, as Bat Chavez walked from the house, Rock swung into the saddle. "Dave!" he yelled at the cook. "You watch over Hardy. We won't be long gone."

Abruptly he swung the stallion south. Chavez rode beside him, glancing from time to time at Rock. Finally he burst out. "Bannon, I think that gal's on the level. I sure do!"

"Yes?" Rock did not turn his head. "You let me worry about that."

CHAPTER NINE

Pike Purcell was a grim and lonely man. He had been loitering all day around the saloon. Only that morning before riding away to the attack on the Bishop ranch house, in which he and Lamport had taken part, Dud Kitchen had told him about the bullet that killed Collins.

Pike was disturbed. His heart had not been in the fight at the ranch, and he had fired few shots. In fact, he and Lamport had been among the first to turn away from the fight. Purcell was thoroughly disillusioned with Mort Harper. The attack on the ranch had been poorly conceived and carried out even more poorly. Purcell didn't fancy himself as a leader, but he knew he could have done better.

Men had died back there—too many of them. Pike Purcell had a one-track mind, and that one track was busy with cogitation over the story told him by Dud. He could verify the truth of the supposition. Mort Harper had been behind Collins. It worried him, and his loyalty, already shaken by inadequate leadership, found itself on uncertain ground.

On the ride back there had been little talk. The party was sullen and angry. Their attack had failed under the straight shooting of Bishop and Bannon. They were leaving six men behind, six men who were stone dead. Maybe they had killed two, but that didn't compensate for six. Bishop was down, but how badly none of them knew.

Cap Mulholland had ridden in the attack as well. Never strongly inclined toward fighting, he had had no heart in this fight. He had even less now. Suddenly he was realizing with bitterness that he didn't care if he ever saw Mort Harper again.

"They'll be comin' for us now," Cap said.

"Shut up!" Lamport snapped. He was angry and filled with bitterness. He was the only one of the settlers who had thrown in completely with Harper's crowd, and the foolishness of it was now apparent. Defeat and their own doubts were carrying on the rapid disintegration of the Harper forces. "You see what I saw?" he demanded. "That Crockett girl was there. She was the one dragged Bishop's body back. I seen her!"

Harper's head jerked up. "You lie!" he snapped viciously.

Lamport looked across at Harper. "Mort," he said evenly, "don't you tell me I lie."

Harper shrugged. "All right, maybe she was there, but I've got to see it to believe it. How could she have beaten us to it?"

"How did Bannon beat us back?" Lamport demanded furiously. "He was supposed to be lost in the hills."

"He must have come back over the mountain," Gettes put in. He was one of the original Harper crowd. "He must have found a way through."

"Bosh!" Harper spat. "Nothing human could have crossed that mountain last night. A man would be insane to try it."

"Well," Pike said grimly, "Bannon got there. I know good and well he never rode none of those cañons last night, so he must've come over the mountain. If any man could, he could."

Harper's eyes were hard. "You seem to think a lot of him," he sneered.

"I hate him," Pike snapped harshly. "I hate every step he takes, but he's all man!"

Mort Harper's face was cruel as he stared at Pike. Purcell had ridden on, unnoticing.

Pike did not return to his cabin after they reached Poplar. Pike Purcell was as just as he was ignorant and opinionated. His one quality was loyalty, that and more than his share of courage. Dud Kitchen's story kept cropping up. Did Harper own a small gun?

Suddenly he remembered. Shortly after they arrived at Poplar he had seen such a gun. It was a .34 Patterson, and Mort Harper had left it lying on his bed.

Harper was gone somewhere. The saloon was empty. Purcell stepped in, glanced around, and then walked back to Harper's quarters. The room was neat, and things were carefully arranged. He crossed to a rough wooden box on the far side of the room and lifted the lid. There were several boxes of .44s, and a smaller box. Opening it, he saw a series of neat rows of .34-caliber cartridges, and across the lead nose of each shell was a deep notch!

He picked up one of the shells and stepped back. His face was gray as he turned toward the door. He was just stepping through when Mort Harper came into the saloon.

Quick suspicion came into Mort's eyes. "What are you doin' in there?" he demanded.

"Huntin' for polecat tracks," Purcell said viciously. "I found 'em!" He tossed the shell on the table. It was the wrong move, for it left his right hand outstretched and far from his gun.

At such a time things happen instantaneously. Mort Harper's hand flashed for his gun, and Purcell was late, far too late. He had his hand on the butt when the bullet struck him. He staggered back, hate blazing in his eyes, and sat down hard. He tugged at his gun, and Harper shot him again.

Staring down at the body of the tall, old mountaineer, Mort Harper saw the end of everything. So this was how things finished? An end to dreams, an end to ambition. He would never own Bishop's Valley now. He would never own the greatest cattle empire in the West, a place where he would be a king on his own range, with nothing to control his actions but his own will.

He had despised Purcell for his foolishness in following him. He had led the settlers like sheep, but now they would survive and he would die. In a matter of hours, perhaps even minutes, Bannon would be coming, and then nothing would be left here but a ruin.

At that moment he heard a pounding of horse's hoofs and looked up to see Sharon go flying past on her black mare.

There was something left. There was Sharon. Rock Bannon wanted her. Sudden resolution flooded him. She was one thing Bannon wouldn't get! Mort Harper ran to his quarters, threw a few things together, and then walked out. Hastily, under cover of the pole barn, he saddled a fresh horse, loaded his gear aboard, swung into the saddle, and started up the cañon toward the Crockett home.

Cap Mulholland watched him go, unaware of what was happening. Dud Kitchen had heard the shots and had returned for his own guns. He watched Harper stop at the Crockett place, unaware of the stuffed saddlebags. When he saw the man swing down, he was not surprised.

Sharon had caught Jim Satterfield in the open and told him they should flee the village at once. At this moment Satterfield was headed for the Pagones' house as fast as he could move. Sharon ran into her house, looking for her father, but as usual he was in the fields. There was not a moment to lose. She ran out and was about to swing into the saddle when Mort Harper dismounted at the front steps. He heard her speak to the horse and stepped around the house.

"Sharon," he said, "you're just in time."

She halted. "What do you mean?" she demanded coolly.

He rushed to her excitedly. "We're leaving! We

must get away now. Just you and me! The Bishop crowd will be coming soon, and they'll leave nothing here. We still have time to get away."

"I'm going to get my father now," she said. "Then we'll go to the hills."

"There's no time for that . . . he'll get along. You come with me!" Harper was excited, and he did not see the danger lights in Sharon's eyes.

"Go where?" she inquired.

Mort Harper stared at her impatiently. "Away! Anywhere for the time being. Later we can go on to California together, and . . ."

"Aren't you taking too much for granted?" She reached for the black mare's bridle. "I'm not going with you, Mort. I'm not going anywhere with you."

It was a real shock. He stared at her, unbelieving and impatient. "Don't be foolish!" he snapped. "There's nothing here for you. You were practically promised to me. If it's marriage you want, don't worry about that. We can go on to California and be married there."

"It is marriage I want, Mort, but not to you. Never to you. For a little while I was as bad as the others, and I believed in you. Then I saw the kind of men you had around you, how you'd deliberately led us here to use us for your own ends. No, Mort. I'm not marrying you and I'm not going away with you." She made no attempt to veil the contempt in her voice. "If you're afraid, you'd better get started. I'm going for my father."

Suddenly he was calm, dangerously calm. "So? It's that Rock Bannon, is it? I never thought you'd take that ignorant cowhand seriously. Or," he sneered, "is it your way of getting Bishop's Valley?"

"Get out!" she said. "Get out now! Dad and Pagones will be here in a moment, and, when I tell them what you've said, they'll kill you."

"Kill me? Those two?" He laughed. Then his face stiffened. "All right, I'll get out, but you're coming with me!"

He moved so swiftly she had no chance to defend herself. He stepped toward her suddenly and she saw his fist start. The shock of the blow was scarcely greater than the shock of the fact that he had struck her. Dimly she realized he had thrown her into the saddle and was lashing her there. She thought she struggled, but she lived those moments only in a half world of consciousness, a half world soon pounded into oblivion by the drum of racing horses. . . .

It was Satterfield who finally got Crockett from the fields. The Bishop riders were already in sight when Tom raced into his house, caught up his rifle, and called for Sharon. She was gone, and he noted that her black mare was gone. She was away, that was the main thing. With Jim, he ran out into the field, where he was joined by Pagones, his wife and daughter, and Dud Kitchen.

The others were coming. It was a flight, and there was no time to prepare or take anything but what lay at hand. Cap Mulholland, his face sullen, went with them, his wife beside him. The Olsens and Greene joined them, and in a compact group they turned away toward the timber along the hillside.

Lamport did not go. He had no idea that Mort Harper was gone. John Kies was in his store, awaiting the uncertain turn of events. Kies had worked with Mort before, and he trusted the younger man's skill and judgment.

It was over. It was finished. Lamport stared cynically at the long buildings of the town. Probably it was just as well, for he would do better in the gold fields. Steady day-to-day work had never appealed to him. Pike Purcell had been an honest but misguided man. Lamport was neither. From the first he had sensed the crooked grain in the timber of Mort Harper, but he didn't care.

Lamport felt that he was self-sufficient. He would stay in as long as the profits looked good, and he would get out when the luck turned against them. He had seen the brilliant conception of theft that had flowered in the brain of Mort Harper. He saw what owning that valley could mean.

It was over now. He had lived and worked with Purcell, but he had no regret for the man. Long ago he had sensed that Harper would kill him someday. Of all the settlers, Lamport was the only one who had read Harper aright, perhaps because they were of the same feeling.

Yet there was a difference. Lamport's hate was a tangible, deadly thing. Harper could hate and he could fight, but Harper was completely involved with himself. He could plot, wait, and strike like a rattler. Lamport had courage with his hate, and that was why he was not running now. He was waiting, waiting in the full knowledge of what he faced.

His hate for Rock Bannon had begun when Bannon rode so much with Sharon. It had persisted, developing from something much deeper than any rivalry over a woman. It developed from the rivalry of two strong men, of two fighting men, each of whom recognizes in the other a worthy and dangerous foe.

Lamport had always understood Harper. Of all those that had surrounded him, Lamport was the only one Mort Harper had feared. Pete Zapata he had always believed he could kill. Lamport was the one man with whom he avoided trouble. He even avoided conversation with him when possible. He knew Lamport was dangerous, and he knew he would face him down if it came to that.

He was a big man, as tall as Rock Bannon, and twenty pounds heavier. When he walked, his head thrust forward somewhat and he stared at the world from pale blue eyes beneath projecting shelves of beetling brows. In his great shoulders there was a massive, slumbering power. Lamport's strength had long since made him contemptuous of other men, and his natural skill with a gun had added to that contempt. He was a man as brutal as his heavy jaw, as fierce as the light in his pale eyes.

Surly and sullen, he made friends with no one. In the biting envy and cantankerousness of Pike Purcell he had found companionship if no more. Lamport was not a loyal man. Purcell's death meant nothing to him. He waited for Rock Bannon now, filled with hatred for the victor in the fight, the man who would win.

Thinking back now, Lamport could see that Rock had always held the winning hand. He had known about Bishop, was a kin to him, had known what awaited here. Also, from the start his assay of Harper's character had been correct.

From the beginning, Lamport had accepted the partnership with Purcell, rode with the wagon train because it was a way West, and threw in with Harper for profit. In it all, he respected but one man, the man he was now waiting to kill.

When he heard the horses coming, he poured another drink in the deserted bar. Somewhere around, there were three or four more men. The rest had vanished like snow in a desert sun. Hitching his guns into place, he walked to the door and out on the plank porch.

John Kies's white face stared at him from an open window of the store.

"Where's Mort?" Kies said. "That's them coming now."

Lamport chuckled and spat into the dust. He scratched the stubble on his heavy jaw and grinned sardonically at Kies.

"He's around, I reckon, or maybe he blowed out. The rest of 'em have."

Stark fear came into the storekeeper's face. "No! No, they can't have!" he protested. "They'll have an ambush! They'll . . ."

"You're crazy." Lamport sneered. "This show is busted. You should know that. That's Bannon comin' now, and, when that crowd of his gets through, there won't be one stick on another in this town."

"But the settlers!" Kies wailed. "They'll stop him."

Lamport grinned at him. "The settlers have took to the hills. They are gone. Me, I'm waitin' to kill Rock Bannon. Then, if I can fight off his boys, I'm goin'."

They came up the street, walking their horses. Rock was in the lead, his rifle across his saddle bows. To his right was Bat Chavez, battle hungry as always. To his left was Red, riding loosely on a paint pony. Behind them, in a mounted skirmishing line, came a dozen hard-bitten Indian-fighting plainsmen, riders for the first big cow spread north of Texas.

A rifle shot rang out suddenly from a cabin in the back of the store, then another. A horse staggered and went down, and Bat Chavez wheeled his horse and with four riders raced toward the cabin. The man who waited there lost his head suddenly and bolted.

A lean blond rider in a Mexican jacket swept down on him, rope twirling. It shot out, and the horse went racing by, and the burly teamster's body was a bounding thing, leaping and tumbling through the cactus after the racing horse. Chavez swung at once, and turned back toward the saloon. The riders fanned out and started going through the town. Where they went, there were gunshots, then smoke.

Rock Bannon saw Lamport standing on the porch. "Don't shoot!" he commanded. He walked the steel-dust within twenty feet. Lamport stood on the edge of the porch, wearing two guns, his dark, dirty red wool shirt open at the neck to display a massive, hairy chest.

"Howdy, Rock!" Lamport said. He spat into the dust. "Come to take your lickin'?"

"To give you yours," Rock said coolly. "How do you want it?"

"Why, I reckon we're both gun handy, Rock," Lamport said, "so I expect it'll be guns. I'd have preferred hand-muckin' you, but that would scarcely give you an even break."

"You reckon not?" Rock slid from the stallion. "Well, Lamport, I always figure to give a man what he wants. If you think you can take me with your hands, shed those guns and get started. You've bought yourself a fight."

Incredulous, Lamport stared at him. "You mean it?" he said, his eyes brightening.

"Stack your duds and grease your skids, coyote," Rock said. "It's knuckle and skull now, and free fighting if you like it."

"Free, he says!" A light of unholy joy gleamed in Lamport's eyes. "Free it is!"

"Watch yourself, boss," Red said, low voiced. "That *hombre* looks like blazin' brimstone on wheels."

"Then we'll take off his wheels and kick the brimstone out," Rock said. He hung his guns over the saddle horn as Bat Chavez rode around the corner.

Lamport faced him in the dust before the saloon, a huge grizzly of a man with big iron-knuckled hands and a skin that looked like a stretched rawhide.

"Come and get it!" he sneered, and rushed.

As he rushed, he swung a powerful right. Rock Bannon met him halfway and lashed out with his own right. His punch was faster, and it caught the big man flushly, but Lamport took it on the mouth, spat blood, and rushed in, swinging with both fists. Suddenly he caught Bannon and hurled him into the dust with such force that a cloud of dust arose. Rock rolled over like a cat, gasping for breath, and just made it from under Lamport's driving boots as the big man tried to leap on him to stamp his life out.

Rock scrambled to his feet and lunged as he picked his hands out of the dust, butting Lamport in the chest. The big renegade jerked up a stiff thumb, trying for Rock's eye, but Bannon rolled his head away and swung a left to the wind, and then a driving right that ripped Lamport's ear, starting a shower of blood.

Lamport now charged again and caught Bannon with two long swings on the head. His skull roaring with pain and dizziness, Rock braced himself and started to swing in a blind fury, both hands going with every ounce of power he could muster.

Lamport met him, and, spraddle-legged, the two started to slug. Lamport was the bigger, and his punches packed terrific power, but were a trifle slower. It was nip and tuck, dog eat dog, and the two battled until the breath gasped in their lungs and whistled through their teeth. Lamport ducked his battered face and started to walk in, stemming the tide of Bannon's blows by sheer physical power.

Rock shifted his attack with lightning speed. He missed a right, and, following it in with the weight of his body, he slid his arm around Lamport's thick neck. Grabbing the wrist with his left hand, he jerked up his feet and sat down hard, trying to break Lamport's neck.

But the big renegade knew all the tricks, and, as Rock's feet flew up, Lamport hurled his weight forward and to the left, falling with his body half across Bannon. It broke the hold, and they rolled free. Rock came to his feet, and Lamport, cat-like in his speed, lashed out with a wicked kick for his head.

Rock rolled away from it and hurled himself at Lamport's one standing leg in a flying tackle. The big man went down, and, as they scrambled up, Rock hit him with a left and right, splitting his right cheek in a bone-deep gash and pulping his lips.

Lamport was bloody and battered now, yet he kept coming, his breath wheezing. Rock Bannon stabbed a left into his face, set himself, and whipped a right uppercut to the body. Lamport gasped. Bannon circled, and then smashed him in the body with another right, and then another and another. Lamport's jaw was hanging open now, his face battered and bleeding from a dozen cuts and abrasions. Rock walked in, measured him, and then crossed a right to his chin. He followed it up with two thudding, bone-crushing blows. Lamport reeled, tried to steady himself, and then measured his length in the dust.

Rock Bannon weaved on his feet, and then walked to the watering trough and ducked his head into it. He came up spluttering, and then splashed water over his face and body, stripping away the remnants of his torn shirt.

"We got 'em all, boss," Red said. "You want we should go after the settlers?"

"No, and leave their homes alone. Where's Kies?"

"The storekeeper? Inside, I guess."

Rock strapped on his guns and strode up the steps of the store with Red and Chavez at his heels. Kies was waiting behind the counter, his face white.

"Kies," Rock said, "have you got the bills for the goods you sold the settlers?"

"The bills?" Kies's frightened eyes showed doubt and then dismay. "Why, yes."

"Get 'em out."

Fumblingly Kies dug out the bills. Quickly Bannon scanned through them. Then he took a match and set fire to the stack as they lay on the counter.

Kies sprang for them. "What are you doing?" he screamed.

"You're payin' the price of hookin' up with a crooked bunch," Bannon said grimly as Chavez held the angry storekeeper. "You got a horse?"

"Yes, I have a . . . horse, but I . . ."

"Red," Bannon turned. "Give this man some shells, a rifle, a canteen, and two days' grub, skimpy rations. Then put him on a horse and start him on his way. If he tries to load that rifle or if he doesn't ride right out of the country, hang him."

"But the Indians!" Kies protested. "And my store!"

"You haven't got a store," Bannon told him harshly. "You'll have to look out for the Indians yourself."

"Boss," Chavez touched him on the shoulder, "*hombre* here wants to talk."

Rock Bannon wheeled. Tom Crockett, Pagones, and Dud Kitchen were standing there.

"Bannon," Crockett said, "Harper took my girl. Kitchen saw him tying her to a horse."

Rock's face went white and then stiffened. "I reckon he was the one she wanted," he said. "She had Zapata waitin' for me, and she led that raid to the ranch."

"No, she didn't do that, Rock," Pagones said. "The raid wasn't even organized when she left. As for Zapata . . ."

"He forced himself on us," Crockett protested. "And she was tied to the saddle. She didn't want to go with Harper. She was in love with you."

"That's right, Rock," Pagones assured him. "Mary's known that for weeks."

"All right," Rock said. He jerked a shirt from a stack on the counter and began getting into it. "I'll find 'em."

"Who goes along with you?" Bat asked eagerly.

"Nobody," Bannon said. "This is my job."

Chapter Ten

The steel-dust stallion liked the feel of the trail. He always knew when he was going some place that was beyond the place where distance lost itself against the horizon. He knew it now, knew in the sound of Rock Bannon's voice and the easy way he sat in the saddle.

Rock rode through the poplars where the wagon train had spent its last night on the trail, and, as he passed, he glanced down at the ruts, already grown with grass. It seemed such a long time ago, yet it was scarcely more than days since the wagons had waited here. He had observed them from the mountains, looking back for the last time as he rode away from the train.

He turned the stallion up the long, grassy cañon where Freeman had been killed. The trail Mort Harper had left was plain enough. So far, he had been running; later, he would try to cover it. Yet Bannon was already looking ahead, planning, trying to foresee what plan, if any, could be in the man's mind.

The Day's River region was one of the most rugged in all America. No man knew it well; few knew it even passingly well. Unless a man chose carefully of the trails that offered, he would run into a blind cañon or end in a jump-off or at some blind tangle of boulders.

There were trails through. The Indians had used them. Other Indians, ages before, had left picture writing on the cañon walls, some of them in places almost impossible to reach. No man knew the history of this region.

There were places here with a history stranger than any written—an old weapon washed from the sands of a creek, a strange date on a cañon wall. There was one place miles from here where the date 1642 was carved on a cañon wall among other dates and names, and no man had yet accounted for that date or said who put it there or how he came to be in the country.

From Grass Cañon the trail of the two horses led into a narrow draw with very steep sides overgrown with birch, balsam, and cottonwood. His rifle ready, although anticipating no trouble at this stage, Rock pushed on.

The draw now opened on a vast region of jagged mountain ridges, gorges, cliffs, and mesas. The stallion followed the trail along the edge of a meadow watered by a brawling mountain stream. Some teal flew from the pool of water backed up by a beaver dam, and Rock heard the sharp, warning slap of the beaver's tail on the water.

The trail dipped now down a narrow passage between great rock formations that towered heavenward. On one side was an enormous mass of rock like veined marble, and on the other a rock of brightest orange fading to rust red, shot through with streaks of purple.

Boulders scattered the space between the walls, and at times passage became difficult. At one place great slabs of granite had sloughed off from high above and come crashing down upon the rocks below. Far ahead he could see the trail leaving the lowlands and climbing, thread-like, across the precipitous wall of the mountain.

Studying the trail and the speed of the horses he was following, Rock could see that Mort was trying for distance, and fast. Rock knew, too, that unless Harper was far ahead, he would, if watching his back trail, soon know he was followed. From the incredible heights ahead, the whole series of cañons and gorges would be plainly visible except when shoulders of rock or boulders intervened.

The trail up the face of the cliff had been hewn by Nature from the solid rock itself, cutting across the face of an almost vertical cliff and only emerging at times in bare rock ledges or dipping around some corner of rock into a cool, shadowed gorge.

"He's headin' for Big Track," Rock told himself suddenly. "He sure is. He's headin' for Big Track Hollow."

He knew the place, and certainly, if Harper was following a known or planned route, he could choose no better. Big Track Hollow was a basin over 6,000 feet above sea level where there was a wealth of grass, plenty of water, and sheltering woods.

It would be the best place in this region to hole up for any length of time. Long ago, somebody had built a cabin there, and there were caves in the basin walls. It took its name from gigantic dinosaur tracks that appeared in the rock all along one side.

For Harper the place had the distinct advantage of offering four separate avenues of escape. Each one would take him over a trail widely divergent from the others, so once a follower was committed to one trail, he would have to retrace his steps and start over again to find his quarry. The time consumed would leave him so far behind that it would be impossible to catch up.

Rock Bannon stared thoughtfully at the tracks. It would soon be night, and the two must stop. Yet they had sufficient lead on him to make it difficult to overtake them soon, and at night he could easily get off the trail and lose himself in the spider web of cañons.

Reluctantly he realized he must camp soon. The landscape everywhere now was rock, red rock cliffs towering against the sky, cathedral-shaped buttes, and lofty pinnacles. He rode down the steep trail, dipping into shadowy depths and riding along a cañon that echoed with the stallion's steps. It was like riding down a long hallway carved from solid rock, lonely and empty.

There was no sound but the walking of the horse and the creak of the saddle leather. Dwarfed by the lofty walls, he moved as a ghost in a vast, unreal world. Yet he rode warily, for at any point Harper might elect to stop and waylay him.

Now the trail down the long avenue between the walls began to rise, and suddenly he emerged upon a plateau that seemed to hang upon the rim of the world.

Far away and below him stretched miles upon miles of the same broken country, but there were trees and grass in the valleys below, and he turned the horse at right angles and then reined in. Here for a space were gravel and rock. He studied the ground carefully, and then moved on.

The trail was difficult now, and in the fading light he was compelled to slip from the saddle, rifle in hand, and walk along over the ground. They wound around and around, steadily dropping. Then ahead of him he saw a pool and beside it a place where someone had lain to drink.

Sliding to the ground, he stripped the saddle from the stallion and tethered him on a grassy plot. Then he gathered dry sticks for a fire, which he made, keeping it very small and in the shadow of some boulders. When the fire was going, he made coffee and then slipped back from the fire and carefully scouted the surrounding darkness.

Every step of the way was a danger. Mort Harper was on the run now, and he would fight like a cornered rat, where and when and how he could find the means.

Before daylight, Rock rolled out, packed his gear, and saddled the stallion. Yet, when it was light enough to see, there was no trail. The water of the stream offered the best possibility, so he rode into it himself, scanning the narrow banks with attention.

Finally, after being considerably slowed down by the painstaking search, he found where they had left the stream. A short distance farther, after seeing no marks, he found a bruised clump of grass where a horse had stepped and slipped.

He had gone no more than four miles when he found where they had camped. There had been two beds, one back in a corner of rocks away from the other, and cut off from the trail by it. Mort Harper was taking no chances. Yet when Rock looked around, he glimpsed something under a bush in the damp earth.

Kneeling, he put his head under the bush. Scratched in the earth with a stick were the words BE CAREFUL and then BIG TRACK.

He had been right then. Harper was headed for Big Track. If that was so, they were a good day's ride from there. Bannon thought that over while climbing the next ridge. Then he made a sudden decision. From the ridge, he examined the terrain before him, and then wheeled his horse. As he did so, a shot rang out. Leaping from the horse to a cleft in the rock, he lifted his rifle and waited.

The country on the other side of the ridge was fairly open, but with clumps of brush and boulders. To ride down there after a rifleman, and Harper was an excellent shot, would be suicide. Only his wheeling of the stallion had saved his life at that moment.

Sliding back from the cleft, he retreated down the hillside to the steel-dust. He swung into the saddle, and, keeping the ridge between him and the unseen marksman, he started riding east. He had made his decision, and he was going to gamble on it.

If he continued to follow, as he was following now, he would fall farther and farther behind, compelled to caution by Harper's rifle and the difficulty of following the trail. If Harper reached Big Track Hollow first, it would be simple for him to take a trail out of there, and then it would be up to Bannon to find which trail.

Rock Bannon had never heard of a cut-off to Big Track, but he knew where he was and he knew where Big Track was. Ahead of him a draw opened and he raced the steel-dust into it and started along it, slowing the horse to a canter. Ahead of him and on the skyline, a sharp pinnacle pointed at the sky. That was his landmark.

The country grew rougher, but he shifted from draw to draw, cut across a flat, barren plateau of scattered rocks and rabbit grass, and traversed a lava flow, black and ugly, to skirt a towering rust-red cliff. A notch in the cliff ahead seemed to indicate a point of entry, so he guided the stallion among the boulders. A lizard darted from under the stallion's hoofs, and overhead a buzzard wheeled in wide, lonely circles.

The sun was blazing hot now, and the rocks caught and multiplied the heat. He skirted the gray, dirty mud shore of a small alkaline lake and rode into a narrow cleft in the mountain.

At one point it was so narrow that for thirty yards he had to pull one foot from the stirrup and drag the stirrup up into the saddle. Then the cleft opened into a spacious green valley, its sides lined with a thick growth of quaking aspen. There was water here, and he stopped to give the stallion a brief rest and to drink.

They had been moving at a rapid clip for the distance and the heat. Yet the horse looked good. Again he checked his guns. It was nip and tuck now. If he were to make Big Track before they reached it, or by the same time, he must hurry. If he failed, then there was not one chance in a dozen that he would ever see Sharon again.

Now every movement, every thought, and every inflection of her voice returned to him, filling him with desperation. She was his. He knew it in every fiber of his being. She was his and had always been his, not only, he understood now, in his own heart, but in hers. He had always known what Mort Harper was. He should never have doubted the girl. It was amazing to him now that he had doubted her even for an instant.

So on he went, although the sun blazed down on the flaming rocks in a torment and the earth turned to hot brass beneath the stallion's hoofs. The mountains grew rougher. There was more and more lava, and then, when it seemed it could get no worse, he rode out upon a glaring white alkali desert that lasted for eight miles at midday, stifling dust and blazing sun.

Rock Bannon seemed to have been going for hours now, yet it was only because of his early start. It was past one in the afternoon, and he had been riding, with but one break, since four in the morning.

On the far side of the desert, there was a spring of water that tasted like rotten eggs—mineral water. He drank a little, rubbed the horse down with a handful of rabbit grass, and let him graze briefly. Then he mounted again, and went on, climbing into the hills.

Big Track was nearer. Somewhere not far from the great sky-stabbing pinnacle he had seen. Sweat streamed down his face and down his body under the new shirt. He squinted his eyes against the sun and the smart of the sweat. He had to skirt a towering peak to get to the vicinity of Big Track.

He was riding now with all thought lost, only his goal in mind, and a burning, driving lust to come face to face with Mort Harper. Somewhere ahead he would be waiting; somewhere ahead they would meet.

The sun brought something like delirium, and he thought again of the long days of riding over the plains, of Sharon's low voice and her cool hands as he wrestled with pain and fever, recovering from the wounds of a lone battle against Indians. He seemed to feel again the rocking roll of the wagon over the rutted, dusty trail, tramped by the thousands heading for the new lands in the West.

Why had he waited so long to speak? Why hadn't he been able to find words to tell the girl he loved her? Words had always left him powerless; to act was easy, but somehow to shape into words the things he felt was beyond him, and women put so much emphasis on words, on the saying of things, and the way they were said.

He swung down from the saddle after a long time and walked on, knowing even the great stallion's strength was not without limit. The wild, strange country through which he was going now was covered with blasted boulders, the rough, slag-like lava, and scattered pines, dwarfish and wind-bedraggled, whipped into agonized shapes by the awful contortions of the wind.

Then he saw the stark pinnacle almost ahead, and he saw, beyond it, the green of Big Track. He climbed back into the saddle again, and mopped the sweat from his face. The big horse walked wearily now, but the goal was reached. Rock Bannon loosened the guns in their holsters, and, grim-faced, he turned down a natural trail that no man had ridden before him, and into the green lush splendor of Big Track Hollow.

The smell of the grass was rich and almost unbelievable, and he heard a bird singing and the sudden whir of wings as some game bird took off in sudden flight. Water sounded, and the gray stallion quickened his pace. He skirted a wide-boled aspen and rode through a grass scattered with purple and pink asters, white sego lilies, and red baneberry. Then he saw the water and rode rapidly toward it.

He dropped from the saddle, taking a quick look around. No human sound disturbed the calm, utter serenity of Big Track. He dropped to his chest on the ground and drank, and beside him, the steel-dust drank and drank deeply.

Suddenly the stallion's head came up sharply. Warned, Rock felt his every muscle tense. Then he forced himself to relax. The horse was looking at something, and the calling of birds was stilled. He got slowly to his feet, striving to avoid any sudden movement, knowing in every muscle and fiber of his being that he was being watched. He turned slowly, striving for a casual, careless manner.

Mort Harper was standing a short distance away, a pistol in his hand. He was thinner, wolfish now, his face darkened by sun and wind, his eyes hard and cruel. Backed in a corner, all the latent evil of the man had come to the fore. Quick fear touched Rock.

"Howdy," he said calmly. "I see you're not takin' any chances, Mort. Got that gun right where it'll do the most good."

Harper smiled, and with his teeth bared he looked even more vulpine, even more cruel. "We both know what it means to get the drop," Harper said. "We both know it means you're a dead man."

"I ain't so sure," Bannon said, shrugging. "I've heard of men who beat it. Maybe I'm one of the lucky ones."

"You don't beat this one," Mort said grimly. "I've come to kill you, man." Suddenly his eyes darkened with fury. "I'd like to know how in blazes you got here!" he snapped.

"Figured you'd head for this place if you knew the country at all," Bannon replied with a shrug. "So I cut across country."

"There's no other trail," Harper said. "It can't be done."

Rock Bannon stared at him coldly. "Where I want to go, there's always a trail," Bannon said. "I make my trails, Mort Harper, I don't try to follow and steal the work of other men."

Harper laughed. "That doesn't bother me, Rock. I've still got the edge. Maybe I lost on that steal, but I've got your woman. I've got her and I'll keep her! Oh, she's yours, all right . . . I know that now. She's yours, and a hellcat with it, but it'll be fun breaking her, and before I take her out of these hills she'll be broken or dead.

"I've got her, and she's fixed so, if anything happens to me, you'll never find her and she'll die there alone. It'll serve both of you right. Only I'm not going to die . . . you are."

"All rat," Rock said coldly. "A rat, all the way through. I don't imagine you ever had a square, decent thought in your life. Always out to get something cheap, to beat somebody, to steal somebody else's work and fancying yourself a smart boy because of it." Rock Bannon smiled suddenly. "All right, you're going to kill me. Mind if I smoke first?"

"Sure!" Mort sneered. "You can smoke, but keep your hands high, or you'll die quick. Go ahead, have your smoke. I like standing here watching you. I like remembering that you're Rock Bannon and I'm Mort Harper and this is the last hand of the game and I'm holding all winning cards. I've got the girl and I've got the drop."

Carefully Rock dug papers and tobacco from his breast pocket. Keeping his hands high and away from his guns, he rolled a cigarette.

"Like thinking about it, don't you, Harper? Killing me quick would have spoiled that. If you'd shot me while I was on the ground, it wouldn't have been good. I'd never have known what hit me. Now I do know. Tastes good, doesn't it, Mort?"

He dug for his matches and got them out. He struck one, and it flared up with a big burst. Rock smiled, and, holding the match in his fingers, the cigarette between his lips, he grinned at Mort.

"Yes," he said, "it tastes good, doesn't it? And you've got the girl somewhere? Got her hid where I can't find her? Why, Mort, I'll have no trouble. I can read your mind. I can trail you anywhere. I could trail a buzzard flying over a snow field, Mort, so trailing you would be . . ."

The match burned down to his fingers and he gestured with it, then, as the flame touched his fingers, he let out a startled yelp and dropped the match. Jerking his hand from the pain—the hand swept down and up, blasting fire!

Mort Harper, distracted by the gesture and the sudden yelp of pain, was just too late. The two guns boomed together, but Mort twisted with sudden shock, and he took a full step back, his face stricken.

Rock Bannon stepped carefully to one side for a better frontal target, and they both fired again. He felt something slug him, and a leg buckled, but he fired again, and then again. He shifted guns and fired a fifth shot. Harper was on his knees, his face white and twisted. Rock walked up to him and kicked the smoking gun from his hand.

"Where is she?" he demanded. "Tell me!"

Mort's hate-filled face twisted. "Go to the devil!" he gasped hoarsely. "You go . . . plumb to the devil!" He coughed, spitting blood. "Go to the devil!" he said again. Suddenly his mouth opened wide and he seemed to gasp wildly for breath that he couldn't get. Then he fell forward on his face, his fingers digging into the grass, as blood stained the mossy earth beneath him.

Rock walked back to the horse, and stood there, gripping the saddle horn. He felt weak and sick, yet he didn't believe he had been hit hard. There was a dampness on his side, but, when he pulled off the new shirt, he saw that only the skin was cut in a shallow groove along his side above the hip bone.

Digging stuff from his saddlebags, he patched the wound as best he could. It was only then he thought of his leg.

There was nothing wrong with it, and then he saw the wrenched spur. The bullet had struck his spur, twisting and jerking his leg but doing no harm.

Carefully he reloaded his gun. Then he called loudly. There was no response. He called again, and there was no answering sound. Slowly Rock began to circle, studying the ground. Harper had moved carefully through the grass and had left little trail. Rock returned for his horse, and, mounting, he began to ride in slow circles.

Somewhere Mort would have his horses, and the girl would not be far from them. From time to time he called. Two slow hours passed. At times, he swung down and walked, leading the stallion. He worked his way through every grove, examined every boulder patch and clump of brush.

Bees hummed in the still, warm air. He walked on, his side smarting viciously, his feet heavy with walking in the high-heeled boots. Suddenly, sharply the stallion's head came up and he whinnied. Almost instantly, there was an answering call. Then Rock Bannon saw a horse, and, swinging into the saddle, he loped across a narrow glade toward the boulders.

The horse was there, and almost at once he saw Sharon. She was tied to the top of a boulder, out of sight from below except for a toe of her boot. He scrambled up and released her, and then unfastened the handkerchief with which she had been gagged.

"Oh, Rock!" Her arms went about him, and for a long moment they sat there, and he held her close.

After a long time she looked up. "When I heard your horse, I tried so hard to cry out that I almost strangled. Then, when my mare whinnied, I knew you'd find us."

She came to with a start as he helped her down. "Rock! Where's Mort? He meant to kill you."

"He was born to fail," Rock said simply. "He was just a man who had big plans, but couldn't win out with anything. At the wrong time he was too filled with hate to even accomplish a satisfactory killin'."

Briefly, as she bathed her face and hands, he told her of what had happened at Poplar. "Your folks will all be back in their homes by now," he said. "You know, in some ways, Lamport was one of the best of the lot. He was a fighter . . . a regular bull. I hit him once with everything I had, every bit of strength an' power an' drive in me, an' he only grunted."

They sat there in the grass, liking the shade of the white-trunked aspens.

"Dud and Mary are getting married, Rock," Sharon said suddenly.

He reddened slowly under his tan and tugged at a handful of grass. "Reckon," he said slowly, "that'll be two of us."

Sharon laughed gaily and turned. "Why, Rock, are you asking me to marry you?"

"Nope," he said, grinning broadly. "I'm tellin' you. This here's one marriage that's goin' to start off right."

The steel-dust stamped his hoofs restlessly. Things were being altogether too quiet. He wasn't used to it.

About the Author

Louis Dearborn LaMoore (1908-1988) was born in Jamestown, North Dakota. He left home at fifteen and subsequently held a wide variety of jobs although he worked mostly as a merchant seaman. From his earliest youth, L'Amour had a love of verse. His first published work was a poem, "The Chap Worth While," appearing when he was eighteen years old in his former hometown's newspaper, the *Jamestown Sun*. L'Amour wrote poems and articles for a number of small circulation arts magazines all through the early 1930s and, after hundreds of rejection slips, finally had his first story accepted, "Anything for a Pal" in *True Gang Life* (10/35). He returned in 1938 to live with his family where they had settled in Choctaw, Oklahoma, determined to make writing his career. He wrote a fight story bought by Standard Magazines that year and became acquainted with editor Leo Margulies who was to play an important role later in

L'Amour's life. "The Town No Guns Could Tame" in *New Western* (3/40) was his first published Western story.

During the Second World War L'Amour was drafted and ultimately served with the U.S. Army Transportation Corps in Europe. However, in the two years before he was shipped out, he managed to write a great many adventure stories for Standard Magazines. The first story he published in 1946, the year of his discharge, was a Western, "Law of the Desert Born" in *Dime Western* (4/46). A call to Leo Margulies resulted in L'Amour's agreeing to write Western stories for the various Western pulp magazines published by Standard Magazines, a third of which appeared under the byline Jim Mayo, the name of a character in L'Amour's earlier adventure fiction.

L'Amour's first Western novel under his own byline was *Westward the Tide* (World's Work, 1950). L'Amour sold his first Western short story to a slick magazine two years later, "The Gift of Cochise" in *Collier's* (7/5/52). Robert Fellows and John Wayne purchased screen rights to this story from L'Amour for $4,000 and James Edward Grant, one of Wayne's favorite screenwriters, developed a script from it. L'Amour retained the right to novelize Grant's screenplay, which differs substantially from his short story. *Hondo* (Fawcett Gold Medal, 1953) by Louis L'Amour was released on the same day as the film, *Hondo* (Warner, 1953), with a first printing of 320,000 copies.

With *Showdown at Yellow Butte* (Ace, 1953) by Jim Mayo, L'Amour began a series of short Western novels for Don Wollheim that could be doubled with other short novels by other authors in Ace Publishing's paperback two-fers. Advances on these were $800 and usually the author earned few royalties. *Heller With a Gun* (Fawcett Gold Medal, 1955) was the first of a series of original Westerns L'Amour had agreed to write under his own name following the success for Fawcett of *Hondo*.

The great turn in L'Amour's fortunes came about when he was signed by Bantam Books. By 1962 he was writing three original paperback novels a year. *All* of his Bantam Western titles came to be continuously kept in print. Independent distributors were required to buy titles in lots of 10,000 copies if they wanted access to other Bantam titles at significantly discounted prices. L'Amour himself comprised the other half of this successful strategy. He dressed up in cowboy outfits, traveled about the country in a motor home visiting with independent distributors, taking them to dinner and charming them, making them personal friends. He promoted himself at every available opportunity, insisting he was telling the stories of the people who had made America a great nation and he appealed to patriotism as much as to commercialism in his rhetoric. There are also several characteristics in purest form that, no matter how diluted they ultimately would become, account in largest measure for the loyal following Louis L'Amour won from his readers: the young male narrator who is in the process of growing into manhood and who is evaluating other human beings and his own experiences; a resourceful frontier woman who has beauty as well as fortitude; a strong male character who is single and hence marriageable; and the powerful, romantic, strangely compelling vision of the American West which invests L'Amour's Western fiction and makes it such a delightful escape from the cares of a later time—in this author's words that "big country needing big men and women to live in it" and where there was no place for "the frightened or the mean."

About the Editor

Jon Tuska is the author of numerous books about the American West as well as editor of several short story collections, *Billy the Kid: His Life and Legend* (Greenwood Press, 1994) and *The Western Story: A Chronological Treasury* (University of Nebraska Press, 1995) among them. Together with his wife Vicki Piekarski, Tuska co-founded Golden West Literary Agency that primarily represents authors of Western fiction and Western Americana. They edit and co-publish forty titles a year in two prestigious series of new hardcover Western novels and story collections, the Five Star Westerns and the Circle Westerns. They also co-edited the *Encyclopedia of Frontier and Western Fiction* (McGraw-Hill, 1983), *The Max Brand Companion* (Greenwood Press, 1996), *The Morrow Anthology of Great Western Short Stories* (Morrow, 1997), and *The First Five Star Western Corral* (Five Star Westerns, 2000). Tuska has also been editing an annual series of short novel collections, *Stories of the Golden West*, of which there have been seven volumes in all.